+ Samantha

The screen door squeaked open, and Mom stuck her head inside. Her face was white, her blue eyes round as marbles. "Reenie's gone."

I froze.

"We've got to find her. It'll be dark soon."

"I—we—where do we start?"

"I'll check the property. You take the road. She can't have gone far." Mom said, but both she and I knew Reenie could disappear into thin air. In a flash.

When Pigs Fly

JUNE RAE WOOD

The Putnam & Grosset Group

A PaperStar Book, published in 1997 by The Putnam & Grosset Group, 200 Madison Avenue, New York, NY 10016.
PaperStar Books and the PaperStar logo are trademarks of The Putnam Berkley Group, Inc. Originally published in 1995 by G. P. Putnam's Sons. Published simultaneously in Canada.
Printed in the United States of America.

Library of Congress Cataloging-in-Publication Data
Wood, June Rae. When pigs fly / June Rae Wood. p. cm.
Summary: Thirteen-year-old Buddy Rae and her best friend Jiniwin do everything together—taking care of Buddy's slow younger sister, parenting egg babies, talking about boys, and dealing with Buddy's family move to a farm outside Turnback, Missouri.
[1. Sisters—Fiction. 2. Family life—Fiction. 3. Friendship—Fiction. 4. Mentally handicapped—Fiction. 5. Schools—Fiction.] I. Title.
PZ7.W84965Wh 1995 [Eic]—dc20 94-42110 CIP AC
ISBN 0-698-11570-8

10 9 8 7 6 5 4 3 2 1

This book is dedicated to Peggy Heil
and The Official June Rae Wood Fan Club
at Ross Elementary School in Topeka, Kansas.
With special thanks to my editor, Refna Wilkin,
who should consider herself hugged.

Contents

When Pigs Fly

ONE
New Mothers

"I'VE BEEN A MOTHER for two hours, and already I'm a nervous wreck," said Jiniwin, pulling back the blue flannel blanket and peeking at her baby boy in its basket. "Thirteen is too young to have all this responsibility."

"Don't I know it," I replied as I closed my locker.

The air in the school was heavy with the scent of burned food, disinfectant, and swarming bodies. A seventh-grade boy, ogling the front of Jiniwin's pink T-shirt, bumped against me. I frowned at him and tightened my grip on the basket that held my baby girl swathed in pink flannel. "Let's get out of here," I muttered to Jiniwin. "Some people have no consideration for new mothers."

"On my way." She slipped her baby—basket and all—into her huge denim purse and slung the purse strap over her shoulder. With a toss of her mane of gold-highlighted brown hair, she started elbowing her way down the hall, graceful as a butterfly fluttering its wings.

I plopped my baby onto my pile of books and plowed after her, knowing that in comparison, I was a tunneling mole. Last year, in seventh grade, my best friend had turned into a beauty, but there'd been no magical change in me. Sometimes strangers even mistook me for a boy, and not just because I had a boy's name.

My short-cropped hair was reddish orange—a cross between Woody Woodpecker's topknot and Howdy Doody. My brother, Jim Bob, said I had the shape of a milk carton, and when he really wanted to get under my skin, he called me "Ella-Short-for-Elephant." I wasn't huge and wrinkly like an elephant. I was just bulgy around the middle, and my jeans were cutting me in two.

Jiniwin, though, was everything I hoped to be. Even her name, Jiniwin Ingles, was musical, poetic, while I was just plain old Buddy Rae Richter, after my grandfather Bud Wray, who died the day I was born.

Outside the junior high building, a gentle breeze riffled my white T-shirt. It was the end of September, and the air was pungent with the scent of mums and marigolds. I couldn't get used to that. Until the foundry closed five months ago, Turnback, Missouri, had smelled like rotten eggs—sulfur, really. Dad said it was the smell of money, and I guess he was right.

Since he'd lost his job, we'd been scratching to make ends meet.

As Jiniwin and I cut across the grounds toward the elementary school to pick up my younger sister, I asked, "Have you named your baby yet?"

"Nope." She did the hair-toss thing again. I knew it was a nervous habit, but it came across as a carefree gesture and boys lapped it up. "I've been too busy trying to protect him," she said. "Sixth hour, Mark Hayes held him upside down to see if he'd messed his diapers, and just before science class, Bobby Steinberg wanted to see if he'd bounce."

I nodded toward my basket. "I kept her in my locker during P.E."

"Shame on you," said Jiniwin, trying to look ferocious. "That child could have wiggled off the shelf and cracked her noggin."

"Well, I couldn't take her out to the softball field."

"And why not?" she demanded, still sporting that same fierce expression.

I couldn't help smiling. For someone who'd been in speech and debate only four weeks, Jiniwin sure had picked up on the melodrama. "Because," I said, "I didn't want a ball smashing her little round skull."

"Then you should have found a baby-sitter. You know what Mrs. Blatterman said. We can't leave these children unsupervised, even for a minute. Whether we're in church, the bathroom, or the grocery store, we have to take them with us."

"I'm going to feel like a total idiot, taking a hard-boiled egg to church."

"That's not a hard-boiled egg," said Jiniwin in a perfect imitation of our family living teacher. "It's a baby. And if it comes back in two weeks with an injury of any kind, you'll fail the whole section on parenting."

I nodded, thinking about the belly button stamp Mrs. Blatterman had used to mark all the students' eggs. "There's no way to pull a switcheroo, either, if we have an accident."

"So we won't have any accidents," Jiniwin said. "I intend to get an A on this project, to make up for the grade I got on my family tree. I still can't believe Blatterman gave me a C."

Sore subject. Jiniwin hated being average at anything, and that C had left her with a two-day headache and an upset stomach.

Tossing her hair back, she went on, "The nerve of that woman, telling me 'the family tree you handed in was nothing but a stick with a few puny branches.' I couldn't just pull my family history out of the air, and after listing the grandmas and grandpas, I didn't know squat. My so-called mother was hardly ever at home, and I guess my father broke all his fingers, because he never returned my calls."

I pictured my family tree, all bushed out with "grands" and "greats." I had so many cousins and second cousins and kissing cousins, when the whole mob got together on holidays, the commotion would just about blow your ears out.

"Hey," said Jiniwin, jabbing me with her elbow, "there goes your heartthrob."

I glanced up in time to see Lonnie Joe Ross, carrying a little egg basket like ours, slip into the side door of the gym.

Jiniwin chuckled. "He's hiding out. Did you see the look on his face when Mrs. Blatterman gave him that egg and called him 'Daddy'?"

"Silly question. When Lonnie Joe's around, my eyes won't focus on anything else. He's a hunk."

"Today that hunk was *eggs-asperated.*"

Laughing, we rounded the corner at Turnback Elementary and saw my sister Reenie sitting on the steps with her teacher aide, Mrs. Houston. They always waited at the side entrance, to avoid the end-of-the-day hassle that was too stressful for Reenie, with her weak heart.

Reenie was sucking her thumb and stroking something in her lap with her short, stubby fingers, as if it were a kitten. I guessed it was Mrs. Houston's purse. Reenie loved purses—her own and everybody else's.

Bent over, with her straight brown hair hiding her face, Reenie looked like a typical six-year-old girl, sitting on the steps in the sunshine. But she wasn't six years old, and she wasn't typical. She was nine, and she'd been born with Down's syndrome. It was caused by an extra chromosome or something, and it had slowed the development of her mind and body.

Reenie spent most of the school day in a special education class, but Mrs. Houston accompanied her to regular classes for art and music. The school called that "mainstreaming." I called it advertising that Reenie could never measure up.

My parents thought it was great that Reenie got to interact with ordinary students, but they didn't know what all went on at school. They didn't hear the snickers and the snide remarks about Reenie, who was always sucking her thumb or singing a made-up song. At home, the songs were a barometer that measured my sister's happiness. At school, they were laughed at, and not just because she couldn't carry a tune.

A smile lit up Reenie's pale face when she spotted us. Carrying a big black leather purse with a silver buckle, she came splay-footed down the steps on her spindly legs. "Hi, s-s-sissy. Hi, Jivven. Come s-see purse. Pretty purse." Her voice was gruff for such a small girl, and her thick tongue affected her speech.

"Yes, it's pretty," I said, "but you'd better give it back to Mrs. Houston, so she can go home."

"Yeah-kay, s-s-sissy." Reenie clambered up the steps, returned the aide's purse, and picked up her own, a green plastic one with yellow stripes. That purse had caused a major headache this morning. Mom was finishing her midnight-to-eight shift at the nursing home, and Dad and I'd had to get Reenie ready for school. Since she'd refused to wear anything that didn't match the purse, I had to iron her green slacks, and Dad had to wash her yellow T-shirt by hand and dry it in the dryer.

Mrs. Houston smiled down at me. "Buddy, if your mother won't mind, I'll bring my old pocketbook tomorrow and give it to Reenie."

"Goody, goody," said Reenie, clapping her hands.

"Mom won't mind. Everybody gives Reenie old purses."

"Okay, then. See you girls tomorrow," Mrs. Houston said, and she disappeared into the school.

Reenie came back down the steps and touched Jiniwin's purse. "Jivven's purse pretty."

"And look what's inside," said Jiniwin, opening it wide. "A baby boy."

Reenie stared at the egg with her slanty blue eyes and wrinkled her forehead in puzzlement.

"Pretend babies. Egg babies," I said, and tilted my basket to show her.

"I hold baby," Reenie said, reaching for Jiniwin's purse.

"I don't think—" I began.

"It's okay," said Jiniwin. She slid her purse strap off her shoulder and hung it on Reenie's. "Be extra careful. Don't bump it or anything."

"I good girl, Jivven. I careful."

"I know you are." Jiniwin slipped an arm around Reenie's waist, and we started up the sidewalk.

"My baby. No cry," sang Reenie, walking along on

tiptoe. The job of caring for that baby was serious business. I smiled. My sister had come a long way. When she was born, the doctors predicted she wouldn't live, and when she proved them wrong, they said she'd never walk or talk. She had so many scars on her chest from surgeries, Mom called her the "Humpty Dumpty baby" because of all the "pieces."

"Mars to planet Earth," said Jiniwin. "Come in, please."

I blinked at her. "What?"

"I said we should draw faces on these little fellows. Doll them up. Give them personalities."

"Oh. Mrs. Blatterman might not like it."

"Why wouldn't she?" asked Jiniwin. "She'll be impressed that we've taken an interest in our children. That's what parents do. Usually."

The last word dripped with sarcasm. Jiniwin's parents had been divorced for three years, and they gave her so little attention it was as though they'd divorced her, too. She'd rebelled by calling them "Frank" and "Paulette" instead of Mom and Dad.

Frank, an auto mechanic, lived in New Jersey now and mailed monthly child support checks, but no letters. Paulette, a court reporter, made good money working at high-powered trials all over Missouri, so Jiniwin had to spend the night at our house at least three times a week. Actually, I thought she was pretty lucky. She had plenty of spending money from her parents and plenty of love from mine.

At the intersection of Main and Gorrell, we stopped

for the light. Two fifth-graders, Tim Maxwell and Donnie Perkins, came up behind us making duck noises. Certain that they were poking fun at Reenie's splay-footed walk, I instinctively balled one hand into a fist.

"Hey, Reenie," said Tim, "you must have a lot of money in that purse, the way you're guarding it."

She grinned and shook her head. "No money. Baby." She held out the purse so they could see.

When the boys peeked inside, they broke up laughing. "That's not a baby," Tim said. "That's an egg. Any fool can see that."

Reenie laughed with them, unaware that they'd insulted her.

"Get lost, twerp," I said, shaking my fist in Tim's face.

"Buzz off," added Jiniwin.

The light changed, and Jiniwin and I grabbed Reenie's arms and steered her across Gorrell. The boys stayed where they were and made squawking noises as they waited to cross Main.

Reenie looked back over her shoulder, and said, "Funny boys."

That really cracked Tim and Donnie up. They started flapping their arms and cackling like a flock of crazy chickens.

"Some kids are so dumb," said Jiniwin.

"I'd like to clobber them," I muttered, "or wring their scrawny necks."

A few minutes later, we reached the entrance to

Turnback Heights subdivision and scanned the bulletin board on the brick gatepost.

"Looks like you still live here," said Jiniwin. It was our standing joke. The homeowners' association didn't allow signs in the yards, so our house and a couple of others up for sale were listed on the board. At first, it had upset me to think of selling out, but when three months passed and nothing happened, I relaxed.

My family lived at the far end of the subdivision, but Jiniwin and Paulette lived near the entrance. As Paulette put it, she'd ended up with the house and the kid after the divorce. Sometimes I wondered which meant more to her—the house or the kid. The house had the same basic floor plan as others of its size in the subdivision, but Paulette had spent a small fortune trying to outdo her neighbors. Her pale-blue house had dark-blue awnings all around the outside, and a king-sized patio out back with a brick barbecue grill that was hardly ever used. All the houses had little windowpanes framing the front doors, but Paulette's was one of the few with stained glass.

Jiniwin headed for the front porch, saying, "Come on. I'll get my craft stuff to decorate the eggs."

Always the worrier, I said, "We'd better go on home, or Mom'll think Reenie's wandered off again."

"Please? I'll hurry. You know I don't like to go in the house alone," Jiniwin said, so Reenie and I went with her.

On the porch, Jiniwin took her purse back long

enough to get her key. While she fumbled with the lock, I pictured her pale-blue living room with its velvety chairs, and her dining room with the mahogany table and the huge, antique globe of the world. For a while after the divorce, whenever Paulette was out of town, Jiniwin pretended to "find" her mother on that globe. It was hinged at the equator, and it was actually a liquor cabinet in disguise.

When Jiniwin got the door open, we stepped onto thick blue carpet in the foyer. The wood paneling on the walls was all but hidden by giant, gold-framed mirrors.

"Mmmmmmm," said Reenie, breathing in the rose-scented potpourri.

I felt my usual twinge of envy that everything here was so fine, but Jiniwin said, "I hate those mirrors. When I see my reflection, I think somebody's in the house."

She and I parked our books on the dining room table. I held tight to Reenie's hand as we headed for Jiniwin's room for the craft supplies, but she pulled away from me and stopped to use the bathroom in the hall.

Jiniwin's room was as pretty and delicate as spun sugar in a cotton candy machine. It was pink from top to bottom, and she had all the things that I could only dream about—a CD player, a cabinet filled with CDs, a closet overflowing with designer jeans and pink shirts and sweaters. Ever since Paulette had said she hated pink, pink had been Jiniwin's favorite color.

On the dresser was an eight-by-ten portrait of Jiniwin and her parents. She said she needed it to look at when Frank called her on the phone, but I think she kept it to irritate her mother, because his phone calls were few and far between.

While Jiniwin rummaged in the closet, I studied the new poster hanging above the bed. It pictured three mice having a tea party on a pumpkin, and the caption read, I'D RATHER SIT ON A PUMPKIN WITH MY FRIENDS THAN ON A VELVET CUSHION ALL BY MYSELF.

"Where'd you get the poster?" I asked.

"Ordered it," Jiniwin answered from the depths of the closet.

"Ordered it? Why?"

"Because it's me. I really would rather sit on a pumpkin with my friends than on a velvet cushion all by myself."

"Right. You've already got the cushion. Maybe I'll get a pumpkin and put you to the test."

"No tests. You'll just have to take my word for it." Jiniwin emerged from the closet carrying a boot box. "Found it," she said. "Before you know it, our babies will have personality plus."

I grinned. I knew the box was loaded with pipe cleaners, feathers, felt, copper wire, Miss Molly's Glue, Magic Markers, you name it. Our babies were in for a major overhaul. "Won't Mrs. Blatterman—"

My words were cut off by a crash, followed by Reenie yelling, "I s-sorry. I s-s-sorry."

My heart did a flip-flop. What if she'd broken a

figurine or a crystal goblet? We raced through the house and found her in the dining room, standing in a puddle of purple liquid and shards of glass from a green bottle. The lid of the big globe was open, and a powerful odor like fermented grape juice permeated the air. Wine, I supposed, although my parents didn't drink and I'd never been around it.

"Juice," Reenie said, clutching Jiniwin's purse under one arm and sucking on her thumb. "I s-sorry."

Since she would have been screaming her head off if she'd seen a drop of blood, I knew she wasn't hurt. I was torn between sympathy for her and embarrassment at her habit of bothering other people's things. It was a problem everywhere we went.

Somehow, some way, I had to make her understand the boundaries of what was hers and what wasn't. But it was hard to know how much pressure to exert to make her mind. Too little, and you got nowhere. Too much, and it was bad for her heart.

"I s-sorry," Reenie said again. She wanted me to forgive her, to tell her everything was all right.

I looked at her trusting moon-face and gave in. "I know, Reenie, but next time, remember, if it's not yours, don't touch it."

"Yeah-kay, s-sissy."

"It's all right," said Jiniwin. "Don't anybody move until I get rid of the glass."

I helped her pick up the pieces, and while she mopped the liquid off the tile with paper towels, I wiped Reenie's feet and legs. "I'll bet that stuff is expensive," I said as I dropped the used towel into the wastebasket. "Will Paulette be mad?"

Jiniwin laughed, and said airily, "She'll never miss it."

"She won't have to miss it. She'll smell it."

"So we'll hide all the evidence. Her Honor, the court reporter, will never know." Jiniwin pulled the plastic liner out of the wastebasket and disappeared out the back door, and I heard her clattering the lid of a trash can. The lack of respect Jiniwin had for her mother bothered me sometimes, but still, she was always good to Reenie, and that counted for a lot.

When Jiniwin came back inside, she put a new liner in the wastebasket and rearranged the bottles in the liquor cabinet. "There," she said, looking smug, "Paulette will think Loverboy Lawyer has been hitting the sauce."

"But what if she doesn't? What if she thinks *you've* been drinking it?"

"Are you kidding? She doesn't think about me at all." Jiniwin tossed her hair back and glanced around, inspecting the room. "Clean as a whistle, Reenie."

"Yeah, Jivven. I s-sorry."

"Don't worry about it," said Jiniwin, chucking her under the chin. "You were too little to remember, but a long time ago, I broke a lamp doing handstands at your house, and I scratched your coffee table with my roller skate. Your mom should have gotten mad, but she didn't."

"Mom's not one to cry over spilled milk," I said.

She'd repaired the lamp with duct tape and colored the scratch with a crayon, and both the lamp and the table were still in our living room.

"Your folks are really great, you know," Jiniwin said.

"I guess so." To tell the truth, they'd been pretty grouchy lately—Dad, because Mom had found a job, and Mom, because she worked hard and crazy hours as an aide at the nursing home.

Jiniwin stared at me. "You *guess* so? I'd trade places with you any day."

"When pigs fly!" I scoffed. "You'd be broke all the time, like me. You'd hate that."

"Money is nice, but it isn't everything."

"Easy for you to say. You get an allowance every week that would choke a mule."

Jiniwin burst out laughing. "Your expressions crack me up. 'When pigs fly' and 'choke a mule.' What's next? Full as a tick?"

"Nervous as a cat," I countered, but by now, I was laughing, too.

"You're crazier than a bedbug."

It was a war of wits, and I thought fast. " 'Cause you live so high on the hog."

Jiniwin rubbed her stomach. "Right now I'm hungry as a bear."

"And grinning like a possum."

"So let's get busy as beavers," she chortled, "and bug on out of here."

As I picked up my books, I saw my sister in the

kitchen with her head stuck in the refrigerator. Rushing in, I said too loud, "Reenie, no! Shut the door!"

She backed out of the fridge so fast, a tub of margarine fell out and bounced at her feet. "I s-sorry," she said, picking up the margarine and handing it to me.

I put the tub back and sighed. "I know, Reenie, but you've got to remember, if it's not yours, don't touch it."

"Yeah-kay," she said, and before I could stop her, she whisked an apple from a bowl on the table and took a bite of it.

TWO

Groucho and Miss Molly

OUR PLAIN WHITE HOUSE wasn't nearly as fancy as Jiniwin's, but just living in the subdivision was enough for me. The address "Turnback Heights" brought with it a certain amount of prestige.

Mom's hobby was gardening, and Dad's was carpentry, and together they'd made our yard a sight to see. Everywhere you looked, marigolds and zinnias were blooming in a rainbow of colors—in the window boxes, inside little picket fences, in the wishing well. Dad had mowed our yard while we were at school, and the sweet smell of fresh-cut grass floated to us on the breeze.

Reenie set Jiniwin's purse on the driveway and squatted down to scoop up a handful of rocks at the edge of the street. "My dollars. Many, many dollars," she sang to herself as she dropped the rocks one at a time into her green purse. I smiled, thinking how little it took to make her happy. In her mind, rocks were as good as money, and she'd decorated our house with them.

"Reenie, your mom's gonna think you've struck it rich," Jiniwin teased. She was always teasing my sister, but not in the cruel way those fifth-grade boys had.

Reenie was too busy singing and picking up rocks to answer. When she had enough dollars, she gathered up both purses and led the way to the house.

A big square nameplate near the door told the world that the Richters lived here. In addition to our name, Mom had painted a border of flowers and the words, "A house is just a house, but a home is filled with love."

Through the clear glass panes framing the door, I saw a stack of newspapers ready for the recycling plant. On top of the heap sat Dad's hammer and my brother Jim Bob's high-top sneakers. That's the way things were at our house—laid back and comfortable. Sometimes, we got a little too comfortable, but I didn't notice it unless Jiniwin was with me.

I opened the door, and we stepped into the foyer, where a path was worn into our brown carpet. Lined up on the floor and turning the corner was a nice neat row of "dollars." Around that corner was the hallway and one of Mom's prized possessions—a wall of graffiti.

Shortly after we'd moved here, Reenie had scribbled some squiggly lines on the paneling with a green crayon, and Mom had been so happy with her first artwork that she'd declared that place the writing wall. Now you could stand in the hallway and see the Richter family history at a glance—rockets sketched by Jim Bob, birthday heights of us kids, the date of "Humpty Dumpty's" last surgery, a heart and initials that signified my parents' eighteenth wedding anniversary.

"Hey, Buddy," Jiniwin said, nodding toward the wall, "be sure and write something about the eggs."

I knew she wanted to write on the wall herself. It was one more small way of rebelling against her mother, who had had every room in their house repainted after Frank moved out. "You can do the honors," I said, "but let's say hi to Mom first."

She was sound asleep in the living room, curled up on the couch with Tripod, our three-legged cat. They were snuggled up under the granny-square afghan, which I thought was old-fashioned but which Mom said hid the lumps on the sofa. She'd had hopes of getting a new living room suite, until the foundry closed. Now that Dad was drawing unemployment and she was slaving away for minimum wage, they managed to make mortgage payments and buy groceries, and that was about it.

Reenie stuck Jiniwin's egg under Mom's nose. "Look, Mom. Baby."

Tripod yowled, and Mom awoke with a start. Staring blankly at the thing in Reenie's hand, she said, "Am I dreaming, or is that an egg?"

"It's an egg. For family living," I said. "We're pretending it's a baby."

"Oh." When Mom tossed back the afghan, I saw she was wearing her favorite old jeans and her "Supermom" sweatshirt. She still had a good figure, but her short hair, red and wiry like mine, was showing some gray, and she'd had worry lines in her forehead since Reenie's last heart surgery in January. It wasn't the medical costs that bothered Mom, though, because Reenie, being disabled, was covered by Medicaid.

"Dod see baby," Reenie said.

Mom set Tripod on the floor. "Your dad's over at Aunt Sage's, fixing a leaky faucet. You can show him the baby when he gets home. . . . Anybody hungry?"

Reenie waved the green purse. "Give you a dollar."

"Keep your money, hon," Mom said as she kissed Reenie's plump cheek. "This one's on me."

We all went into the kitchen, being careful not to touch Mom's one-and-only white uniform drying in the doorway. To me, that uniform was a comforting sight. When it was gone, Mom was at work, and her absence left a hole in the family.

A kettle bubbled on the stove and a pan of peach surprise sat on the table. The "surprise" was that you poured boiling peaches on top of the batter and the ingredients mixed while they baked. It was Mom's specialty nowadays, since it took little time to make. It was also one of my weaknesses, and I could have eaten the whole panful by myself.

"Irene," said Jiniwin, "your house always smells so good."

"It's just spaghetti sauce, but I'm glad you like it. Your mother called and said she'll be late, so you're eating supper with us."

Jiniwin slumped into a chair. "What's her excuse this time?"

"I don't know. She didn't say."

"Doesn't matter anyway," sighed Jiniwin. "She's not really at home when she's home. She's got that lawyer boyfriend on the brain."

"Single women do get lonely, you know," Mom said.

I wondered why she'd hold up for Paulette, an old school chum who didn't appreciate all the things Mom did for her.

Mom dished up the surprise and didn't even ask about school, which was a surprise in itself. I knew she'd been concerned about money lately, but in the last couple of weeks or so, she'd gotten worse—forgetting where she'd put something, or spacing out in the middle of a conversation.

I chattered away about the events of the day. Usually, Mom wanted a blow-by-blow account of everything. This afternoon she didn't so much as lift an eyebrow when I said one of the cooks had left an oven on all night and baked a batch of brownies to charcoal.

She perked up a little when Jiniwin and I explained about the eggs. "If you ask me, Mrs. Blatterman has a good idea," she said. "When kids realize just how much trouble it is to take care of an egg, maybe they'll think twice before doing something that could get them a real baby."

I finished my snack, but the pan of surprise, all gooey and warm, was begging me to take a second helping. I *had* to get out of this kitchen. Pushing myself away from the table, I did some tall coaxing, trying to get Reenie to turn over Jiniwin's purse with the egg. It didn't work.

"My baby," she said, clutching the purse with both hands.

"You've done a good job baby-sitting, but now Jiniwin wants to take care of her own baby."

"My baby," declared Reenie.

"Come on," I pleaded. "We need the baby now."

"My baby. Give you a dollar."

"I don't want a dollar. I want the baby."

"My baby." Reenie's mouth trembled, like she might cry.

Mom sighed, went to the refrigerator, and took out an egg, which she showed to Reenie. "Give Jiniwin her baby, hon, and I'll make one just for you."

"Here, girl," Reenie said, thrusting the purse at Jiniwin.

Jiniwin took it, then dug out a quarter and laid it in front of my sister. "For you, for baby-sitting."

"You're spoiling her," I said, but I was pleased at her humoring Reenie.

"We all spoil her," Mom observed, and she put the egg on to boil.

Jiniwin picked up the bread sack on the counter. "Irene, may I have a slice?"

"Sure, but if you're still hungry, you can have some more surprise."

"It's for my egg," explained Jiniwin.

"Your egg? Why?" I asked as she pulled out a piece of bread.

"You'll see." She led the way down the hall, stopping long enough to scrawl, "Buddy and Jiniwin, new mothers, Sept. 29," in pink Magic Marker high up on the writing wall.

I followed her into the bedroom I shared with Reenie, my favorite room in the whole house. Gold carpet, light-blue walls, medium-blue furniture. The purses hanging from the dresser knobs and the neat rows of rocks on every flat surface gave the room its own special Reenie touch.

Only when I saw it through Jiniwin's eyes did I notice the flaws—that the carpet was faded, the twin beds didn't match, and the paint on the furniture was chipped because of all the rocks.

"Many dollars," said Jiniwin, grinning at Reenie's handiwork on the dresser.

We kicked off our shoes, sat cross-legged on my bed, and sketched how we wanted our eggs to look. I drew a sweet face with closed eyes and tiny lashes, rosy cheeks, and little tufts of hair. When I saw Jiniwin's drawing, I nearly swallowed my teeth. "Jiniwin Ingles, you can't decorate your egg as Groucho Marx."

She twiddled her pencil as if it were Groucho's cigar. "And why not?"

"Because. It's—it's—"

"It's terrific," said Jiniwin, pouring some Miss Molly's Glue onto the bread.

"It's terrible." I made a face as she squeezed the bread and glue together.

"At least it's original. Every baby in the world looks like yours."

"Does not. Some babies are dog-ugly. This one's cute. I'm going to name her Rosebud."

"Rosebud? Ick! Too corny." Jiniwin kneaded the goopy bread. When it was the right consistency, she tore off a chunk and rolled it between her palms to make a dough ball. "Groucho's nose," she said, jabbing it into place.

Clever. I watched as she drew big black googly eyes and made a pair of spectacles out of copper wire. By the time she'd glued on black feathers for the hair, eyebrows, and mustache, the egg was a dead-ringer for Groucho Marx.

I wadded up my drawing and tossed it behind the bed. After Groucho, anything I came up with would be ho-hum.

"What's the matter?" asked Jiniwin.

"I've changed my mind. I want a baby with character. I just don't know *what* character."

"Maybe just make some neat designs, like we did on Reenie's Easter eggs."

I snapped my fingers. "That's it!"

"What's it?"

"I'll turn my egg into an egg—Humpty Dumpty."

"Humpty Dumpty's a boy."

"Not this time." I grabbed a fine-line marker and drew squiggly cracks across the surface of my egg. I gave her a dough-ball nose and ears, wire-hoop earrings, blue eyes with thick lashes, and a plume of orange hair. When I was finished, I danced her over in front of Jiniwin and said in a sultry voice, "Hi there, big boy. My name's Humpty Dumpty, but all the king's men call me . . ." I paused to think of a good name, and my eyes fell on the glue bottle. "Miss Molly, 'cause I've got it all together again."

Jiniwin and I burst out laughing, and laughed until our sides hurt. We were still at it when the door opened and Mom glanced in. "Reenie's not here?"

"No," I said.

"She was with Tripod in the kitchen not five minutes ago, putting her egg baby in my old flowered purse."

"Maybe she took it over to show Aunt Sage," I suggested.

"I'll call," Mom said, and left.

I crawled off the bed. "We'd better get our shoes on, just in case."

"I know," replied Jiniwin. "They don't call her 'the Flash' for nothing."

The Flash was Jim Bob's nickname for Reenie, because she was a master at disappearing. No matter how long or hard we talked to her, she left the house when she felt like it.

Jiniwin and I were tying our sneakers when Mom came rushing back. "She's not there."

My eyes locked with Mom's only for an instant. It wasn't necessary to discuss our search pattern—we were old hands at searching. She'd look in the subdivision, and I'd look outside of it.

The three of us shot from the house as if there'd been a bomb scare. Jiniwin and I headed toward the entrance gates, keeping our eyes peeled for any sign of Reenie. She could be anyplace. Last summer, I'd found her crying in the park, because someone had tossed her purse into the duck pond. Another time, I'd found her eating a chicken leg she'd gotten who-knows-where.

As we trotted through the gates, I said, "Chances are, she's okay," to reassure myself and ease the tightening in my chest. But my mind whirled with the dangers—railroad tracks, a busy intersection, and kids who liked to taunt, not to mention Reenie's habit of talking to everybody, stranger or not.

It wasn't hard to follow her trail. There weren't many little girls in Turnback, Missouri, with Down's syndrome, an egg in a purse, and a three-legged cat. A lineman on a pole had seen Reenie going east. The lady at the fruit market had given her a banana.

Before long, I zeroed in on her destination. "She's headed for the video store."

"I bet you're right," said Jiniwin. "She likes the clerks."

They liked Reenie, too, and that was part of the problem. They'd once let her rent a movie for a "dollar," and even though Mom convinced them they shouldn't do that anymore, Reenie still went down there and tried.

As we waited for the light at Main and Gorrell, I shuddered at the idea of her crossing that busy street. A couple of times, I'd caught her in the middle of it, directing traffic.

At Vera's Video, we found Reenie watching *Bambi* with Vera, a gray-headed beanpole of a woman. My sister was eating popcorn, with Tripod curled up at her feet. I felt weak-kneed with relief.

"Hi, s-s-sissy. Cartoons." Reenie flashed me a smile so innocent, I could almost see the halo around her head.

"Reenie Richter," I said, "you're in trouble now."

She cocked her head and grinned some more and offered me the popcorn. "Bite?"

"Don't change the subject. You know you're not supposed to leave the yard."

"I've been trying to call your house," Vera said, "but nobody answered."

"We were out searching for the Flash."

Vera chuckled and handed me Reenie's flowered

purse with a banana sticking out. "An egg and a banana," she said. "That's quite a combination."

I was explaining about the egg baby when Jiniwin smacked her forehead and said, "Some mothers we are! We left Groucho and Miss Molly in the house alone."

I frowned. "Let's hope Mrs. Blatterman doesn't find out. Come on, Reenie. Let's go."

"Cartoons," she replied, cramming a handful of popcorn into her mouth.

"You can watch TV at home," I said.

Her eyes never left the screen. "Cartoons."

Vera punched the "pause" button on the control, and the picture went fuzzy.

Reenie stopped chewing and blinked her slanty eyes at Vera. "Cartoons. Give you a dollar."

Vera lifted her eyebrows and looked wise. "Listen!" she said. "Do you hear it?"

We all listened. I heard ice falling in the ice machine and a car going by outside.

"This baby is crying," said Vera. "It's all tuckered out and wants to go home."

Reenie took the purse and peeked inside it. "No cry," she crooned. "No cry."

"Better take it home and put it to bed," Vera said.

"Yeah-kay." My sister leaned over and planted a buttery kiss on her cheek. " 'Bye, Vera. You're a s-s-sweetie-pie."

• • •

On the way home, we saw Lonnie Joe Ross pedaling toward us on his bike. Jiniwin nudged me and said, "Now's your chance. Say something to him."

"No." My tongue always got tangled up when I tried to talk to boys, and especially Lonnie Joe. My eyes worked fine, though, and I couldn't stop looking at his curly black hair blowing in the breeze. He wasn't close enough yet for me to see the cool green of his eyes and that cute little gap between his teeth, but just thinking about them made my heart beat faster.

"Do it," urged Jiniwin.

"He's not interested," I said, tugging self-consciously at the tail of my T-shirt. "I'd have to stand on my head and stack BB's for him to notice me."

"Girl, you've got to learn to flirt. I'll get him over here, and you—"

"No!" I croaked. "We need to let Mom know we've found Reenie."

But she was already flagging him down. "Yo, Lonnie Joe!" she yelled. "How's it going?"

He skidded to a stop and almost wrecked, because he was using one hand to steady the egg in his bike basket. "This little booger is gonna get me killed," he said, grinning at her. "Where's your egg?"

Before she could answer, Reenie said, "Look, boy," and opened her purse to show him.

After a quick glance at her egg, Lonnie Joe knitted

his thick black brows and peered at my sister. Finally, he winked at Jiniwin and said, "Must be something in the water, with all these people having babies."

I felt myself blush to the roots of my hair, but Jiniwin acted as if talking to a boy about having babies was the most natural thing in the world. "Then we'd better switch to Coke," she said.

"Sounds good to me. Well, gotta go. See you tomorrow." Lonnie Joe pushed off on his bike and sailed away. He hadn't once looked at me.

" 'Bye, boy," Reenie called after him, but he must not have heard, because he didn't respond.

"Buddy Richter," said Jiniwin, "you're head over heels for that guy. How come you always clam up when he's around?"

I shrugged.

"All you've got to do is open your mouth and let the words out."

"That's not easy for a milk carton," I said.

"Oh, stop. That brother of yours—"

"Said I should get letters stamped on my forehead and have myself dipped in wax."

"Since when did you start paying attention to Jim Bob?"

I shrugged again.

When we got home, we saw Mom knocking at the Fergusons' house, way down the street. Not finding Reenie in a yard somewhere, she'd evidently tried going door to door.

I yelled at her, and she came jogging toward us.

"Reenie," she panted when she reached the yard, "what am I going to do with you if you keep running off?"

"Baby cry. Bed," said my sister, heading for the house.

We followed her, and Mom sighed in defeat. "I'm scared to spank her, on account of her heart. Sitting her in the corner doesn't work. And I can't ground a child who won't stay grounded. Maybe she'll stop running away after—"

"After what?" I asked.

"Never mind. I shouldn't have said anything yet."

Jiniwin and I gave each other the what's-that-supposed-to-mean? eye signals, but we both knew my mom wasn't going to say any more at the moment.

Reenie had discovered Groucho and Miss Molly in our room, and she came flying down the hall and into the foyer. "My baby. Eyes," she said, wanting a face on her egg, too.

"Not now." I was tired and grumpy and sick of eggs.

"Please, s-sissy. Give you a dollar." Reenie's thumb went to her mouth, and her eyes shone with trust.

There's something almost magical about Reenie. She has a way about her that can melt my heart and brighten my darkest mood. "Oh, all right," I said, hugging the sister who loved me, chub and all. "How'd you like a little girl named Rosebud?"

THREE
The Bomb

"GOOD SPAGHETTI, MOM," said Jim Bob, laying down his fork with a clatter.

"Obviously," I said. "You ate three helpings, and you've got another one on your shirt." When he glanced down at his chest, I said, "Gotcha!"

"Shame on you, Buddy," laughed Jiniwin, who had a massive crush on my sixteen-year-old brother. To her, he was tall and blond and handsome, even in his lime-green car-wash shirt.

Jim Bob winked at her. "Don't worry, Jin. I'll get even with Ella." He left off the Short-for-Elephant part, like he always did when our parents were around.

"Ella?" said Dad, wrinkling his forehead. "Who's Ella?"

"It's me, Dad. He calls me—"

"May I be excused?" interrupted Jim Bob. "I want to shoot baskets with Brian."

He was already out of his chair, but Dad stopped him. "Wait a minute, son. Your mother and I have an announcement to make."

Nodding toward Groucho and Miss Molly on the counter, Jim Bob said, "I already know. You're grandparents, right?"

Dad leaned back and stretched out his long legs. He was broad-shouldered and lean, and water droplets glistened in his slicked-back brown hair. "Sit down, son. This is serious."

Jim Bob shot me a questioning look as he sat back down.

"Irene, should I leave?" asked Jiniwin.

"No. You're like one of the family, so this will affect you, too."

I glanced uneasily at Mom, then at Dad. From the expressions on their faces, they were building up to something I didn't want to hear.

"You know when my great-aunt Ruby died," Dad said, "she left me her farm."

Of course, we knew that. It was a family joke. Aunt Ruby had left Dad a few acres of land with some dilapidated outbuildings and a house. The house was old and ugly, even before Aunt Ruby tacked a hog shed onto it. The last time I'd seen the place, there were hogs snuffling and wallowing outside the living room window. The smell was awful.

"Since I've been laid off, we've been going in the hole pretty fast," Dad said, reaching for a cigarette in the pocket of his chambray shirt. He'd given up smoking a while back, but he still hadn't kicked the habit. To hide his mistake, he began buttoning and unbuttoning the pocket flap. "What it boils down to is, we've got to let this house go and move to the farm."

The words were a bomb, dropped dead-center on the table. Jiniwin and I sat staring at each other, bug-eyed and openmouthed.

"Move?" exclaimed Jim Bob. "All right!"

I glared at him. The farm wasn't worth the matches it would take to set it on fire. "Give up this house for that old shack?" I finally squeaked at Mom.

Her eyes were watery. "Buddy, we've got a potential buyer, and considering how slow the real estate market is, we'd be stupid to turn down his offer. We can't keep up taxes on two places and payments on this one."

"So sell the farm," I cried, "not our *home*!"

"The farm's been on the market for ages, without any takers. You know that," Mom said. "Aunt Ruby's house won't be so bad."

"When pigs fly," I muttered.

Dad shifted in his chair. "When we stop making payments on this house, we'll have a little extra money to fix up Ruby's." He was still fooling with the flap on his shirt, and his eyes had the same wounded look I'd seen when the foundry closed. Dad had a lot of pride, and it was hurting today.

But mine was, too. "There's no hope for that place," I said. "It's creepy and smelly and about a hundred miles from civilization." I could see myself wasting away out there, shriveling up into a wacky old maid like Aunt Ruby.

"It's only four miles from Turnback," said Mom.

I blinked at her. "That's four miles from Jiniwin's house and the theater and the skating rink."

"And the park and the video store and everyplace else that appeals to Reenie's wanderlust," Mom added.

"Cartoons," said Reenie, clapping her hands.

"See?" Mom said. "It's a miracle she hasn't been kidnapped already, or hit by a car or a train. She'll be safer out of town."

How could I argue with that? I sat drawing swirls with my fork in the tomato sauce on my plate.

"James, was your Aunt Ruby really wacky?" Jiniwin asked Dad. If she hadn't been so far away, I'd have kicked her under the table.

"I guess we all know where you got that idea." Dad's voice was bristly, and I could feel him staring daggers at me. " 'Wacky' is a label, just like 'retard,' " he said. "Labels lump people into one big category instead of giving them individual hearts and souls."

I kept working on those swirls.

"Ruby was a good person," Dad went on. "She spent years as a missionary nurse in foreign countries. Even after she came back to Missouri, she devoted her life to helping others, until she got sick."

My brain conjured up an image of Aunt Ruby in a starched housedress and bibbed apron. Long ago, in a kitchen fragrant with pies and homemade bread, she'd sat me down at a round oak table with a magnifying glass, a muffin pan, and a jar of buttons. I'd been in glory sorting them—some big and sturdy, some with rhinestones in the center, and some as delicate as a baby's tooth. That happy memory faded, though, when I recalled the mess Aunt Ruby had made of the house. The Aunt Ruby I loved had died long before her funeral. She'd died the day something inside her head snapped.

"Hey!" exclaimed Jim Bob, and he smacked the table so hard, I nearly fell out of my chair. "Now we can fix up Aunt Ruby's old pickup. Out in the boonies, there aren't any rules against doing mechanic work in the driveway."

"I thought of that, too," Dad replied. "We'll need a second set of wheels."

Jim Bob's eyes gleamed. "When do we move?"

"Next week," said Mom.

"Next week?" I howled. "What's the big rush?"

Mom dabbed at some crumbs on the table with her finger. "Our buyer's being medically discharged from the Army, and he has to move his family soon. He chose Turnback because it's close to the hospital at Whiteman Air Force Base. He'll buy our place if he can take possession in two weeks."

I groaned. "Please, Mom, can't we just—"

"No, we can't, and stop arguing. You might as well

get used to the idea. You'll see it won't be so bad, after we've gone out this weekend and done some cleaning."

"Can I go, too?" asked Jiniwin.

Please, no, I pleaded silently with Mom. Jiniwin's got awnings at her windows. Aunt Ruby's got a *hog shed.*

"You can go if you're willing to work," Mom said. "It'll take a ton of elbow grease to make the house livable."

Jiniwin flexed her muscles, and everybody laughed but me. I narrowed my eyes at her, and asked, "Aren't you forgetting something?"

"What?"

"Like where you're going to stay when Paulette's not around. You hate being home by yourself."

"Oh." Jiniwin twirled a lock of hair. "Well, can't I just ride the school bus home with you?"

"Absolutely *nobody* we know rides a school bus. Mary Jo comes to town with her father thirty minutes early, just so she won't have to."

Frowning, Jim Bob said, "I'm too old to ride a school bus."

"What are you griping about?" I snapped, feeling the need to lash out at somebody. "Since you work after school, you'll only have to ride it in the mornings."

He gave me a grin of maddening superiority and clutched an imaginary steering wheel. "And not at all when we get that pickup running. I'll be chugging down the road while you're still trying to find a seat on the bus."

Terrific. I'd never hear the end of it after he got those wheels.

"Treat me right, Ella, and maybe I'll drive you to school once in a while." Jim Bob jumped up, pretended to slam-dunk a basketball, and breezed out the back door.

His grand exit set everyone in motion but me. Mom and Reenie left for Aunt Sage's with some peach surprise. Dad went in to watch the evening news. Jiniwin started cleaning off the table.

I stayed rooted to my chair. I could see Dad through the doorway, sitting in his easy chair and fumbling with his pocket. I wanted to yell at him that he'd quit smoking, then smash a plate against the wall. But Dad didn't like theatrics and back talk. Me throwing a tantrum would be as productive as him reaching for a cigarette in an empty pocket. It would also get me grounded for life.

Jiniwin was running water into the sink and reaching into the cupboard for the dishwashing liquid. As usual, she was making herself at home.

Grudgingly, I got up to rinse the dishes. While we worked, she yammered on about country living. I didn't need optimism. I needed sympathy—tons of it. "Look," I said at last, "I can't stand this. The way you're carrying on, you'd think we were moving to a dude ranch or something."

She wiped her face with the back of her hand,

leaving soapsuds on her cheek. "Buddy, I hate it that you have to move. I'm just trying to make you feel better, like you did for me with the divorce."

The tears I'd been holding back sprang to my eyes. "Was I as cheerful as you?"

"Worse." She squeezed me with a wet, soapy hug, then turned to scrub the spaghetti sauce pan. "What'll I do when you're not just down the street? With Frank in New Jersey and Paulette always hanging out with that lawyer, sometimes you're the only family I've got. Wish I could move out to the wilderness with you."

"You'd hate it," I said, but it felt good to have her sharing my misery. "Aunt Ruby's house is in terrible shape."

Jiniwin pulled the plug in the sink and began rinsing out the suds with the sprayer. "Does it have indoor plumbing or an outhouse?"

"Plumbing, thank goodness."

"Electricity or kerosene lamps?"

"Electricity, but—"

"How about a telephone?"

"I suppose we'll get one hooked up."

"Indoor plumbing, electricity, and a telephone. What more could a girl want?"

Might as well level with her, I thought as I dried my hands on a towel. Let her know from the start that Aunt Ruby's house is a disgrace to the family. "Dad calls it a farm, but it hasn't been a farm since Aunt Ruby went off her rocker. One summer she fired her hired man, sold her cows, and—" I stopped in mid-sentence to toss the towel to Jiniwin. "Moved her pigs right up next to the house."

"She did what?" she asked, so surprised she missed the towel.

"You heard me. Not a sunporch, not a patio, but a hog shed attached to the house."

FOUR
Going Nowhere Fast

JINIWIN AND I WERE MOPING on the back steps with Groucho and Miss Molly in our laps. Behind us in the kitchen, we could hear Mom talking to the real estate salesman on the phone. Her voice sounded sad, resigned, as if she didn't want to leave our home any more than I did.

I sat looking up at the maple tree that was already changing colors. I wouldn't be here to see it after it became a mass of glorious red. I wouldn't be able to relax in the tree house ever again.

Jiniwin must have read my mind. "Remember when we had our secret club up there and sent messages with the pulley?" she asked.

"Yeah. Back then, we worried about who was bringing the peanut butter, and whether Jim Bob would intercept our notes."

Jiniwin smoothed Groucho's feathery hair away

from his face. "Buddy, how did things get so complicated?" Lowering her voice, and with a glance over her shoulder to see that no one was near the back door, she answered her own question. "It's grown-ups who've caused the problems. It's grown-ups who get divorced, close factories, sell houses. Kids don't have anything to say about any of it. They just have to go along."

"I know," I sighed. "And the grown-ups tell us we live in a democracy."

"That's exactly what I said to Goomer last week."

I nodded. Goomer was an iguana, one of many animals in our science teacher's living lab. The teacher often sent troubled students in alone to see the critters. Talking to them was supposed to calm a person and bring out gentle feelings. Jiniwin went when she was mad at her mother, or when she missed her dad. I went only when it was our class's turn to do the feeding.

"I've got the fidgets," said Jiniwin, standing up. "Let's ride our bikes up to the park and check out the scenery."

By "scenery," she meant boys, and I didn't need that pressure on top of everything else. "You go," I said. "I'll stay here and baby-sit."

"Oh, no, you won't. Exercise is good for depression, and Miss Molly could use the fresh air."

She had that look in her eye that she gets when she's determined to have her way, so it would have been a waste of breath to argue. We fetched our bikes, put our eggs in the baskets, and rode off.

Her bike was a ten-speed, and mine was a me-speed, plus I was hauling all that flab. When we reached the park, I felt sweaty and disheveled. Jiniwin was just the opposite. Her rosy cheeks matched her T-shirt, and she had the windswept hair of a fashion model.

We strolled across the grass with our eggs. When we spotted some ninth-graders playing touch football, Jiniwin grabbed the tail of my shirt and pulled me over in their direction.

Pretty soon, the guys stopped playing and came over to talk. Although Jiniwin kept finding ways to drag me into the conversation, it was obvious the boys had eyes only for her. After a while, feeling as insignificant as a milk carton, I just leaned against a wall and looked homogenized. It was a relief when we headed home.

"Buddy Richter," said Jiniwin as we pedaled along, "you'll never catch a boy if you don't loosen up."

"I can't help it. You're Miss America. I'm Miscellaneous."

"Don't be silly. You've got gorgeous green eyes and thick red hair that doesn't need fixing all the time. I spend half my life using a blow dryer and hot rollers."

"And the other half, you've got great hair, great clothes, and a great body." I dropped one hand from the handlebars and pinched some skin at my waist. "You don't have a spare tire like me."

"So you're a few pounds overweight. Big deal. Your trouble is, you've let Jim Bob get your goat." Jiniwin chuckled. "Did you catch that? Get your goat? That's almost as good as choke a mule."

I laughed. "You're impossible."

"I know. . . . Race you to the gates," she said, and shot ahead of me, pedaling so fast I couldn't catch her.

When I reached the gates of Turnback Heights, she was waiting for me. "Straight home or around the horn?" she asked.

"Around the horn" was Reenie's expression, and it meant circling around through the whole subdivision, rather than cutting straight across to home. "Around the horn," I wheezed. "Enjoy it while I can."

As we rode side by side through the Heights, I was keenly aware of the hum of lawnmowers, the smell of steaks on grills, the creak of swings on porches, the singsong voices of girls jumping rope. This evening, all those little slices of life added to my melancholy. Out in the country, we'd be isolated from the world. There'd be no sights and sounds and smells associated with other people's lives.

It was dusk when we reached my backyard, and we heard a rumbling in the house that signaled Reenie was rolling cans.

"Sounds like we'll have to brave the minefield if we want to get a drink," Jiniwin said, jumping off and kicking the stand on her bike.

We found Reenie sitting cross-legged on the kitchen floor, removing cans from the cupboard and shooting them across the tile like silver bullets. Her eyes were sparkling, her tongue hanging out.

"Hold it, Reenie," I yelled. "We need some Kool-Aid."

"Yeah-kay, s-sissy," she said, but there was no letup of the speeding cans.

A minute later, all the cans were on one side of the kitchen, and she started scooting across on her rump to roll them back.

Jiniwin and I scrambled for the Kool-Aid, filled a couple of glasses, and got out.

In my room, we sat on my bed. Glancing toward the window, Jiniwin said, "Remember when I fell out of the tree house and broke my arm? It was the day after I got locked in your closet."

I sipped at my Kool-Aid. "Yeah. And the next week, we set up that lemonade stand at the entrance gates and got closed down by the association before we could sell the first drop."

We kept on reminiscing until Jiniwin said, "Listen to us. We sound like two old ladies ready to kick the bucket. It's not the end of the world. You're just moving four miles away. That's less than half an hour by bike."

I stared at our reflections on the window glass. One beauty queen, one milk carton. "By the time I've hauled my carcass four miles over hills and dirt roads," I said, "I won't have enough energy left to spit."

"Well, that's a relief. I wouldn't want to hang around with somebody who rode into town just to spit."

We were giggling when Reenie came in, hauling Tripod under her arm and singing, "My kitty. My boy."

The cat, folded in half at the belly, looked like he might break in two, but he was purring as if that were the only way to travel. He was a dull, brain-colored gray, and he'd been born minus one leg. I remembered feeling sorry for him back then, the pitiful brother of four fluffy, fur-ball kittens. He and Reenie had chosen each other, as if they'd both known that perfect wasn't necessarily the best. Mom said it was a match made in heaven, and she was right. Tripod had flourished under Reenie's loving attention, and he'd been her constant companion. In January, coming out from under the anesthetic after surgery, the first thing she'd asked for was her cat.

"Posh," she said as she dumped Tripod on my bed.

"After homework," I said.

"Give you a dollar."

"Let's see the dollar," said Jiniwin, and when Reenie paid off with a rock, Jiniwin scrounged around in her purse and found a bottle of flamingo-pink nail polish.

"Posh." Reenie smiled and climbed up to watch Jiniwin polish the cat's toenails. When his toes were all tipped with bright pink, she splayed out her short, stubby fingers and got herself poshed, too.

"Beautiful," Jiniwin said, blowing on Reenie's nails and replacing the lid on the bottle.

Reenie patted her on the head. "You're a s-sweetie-pie."

"Maybe so, but I'm keeping the dollar," Jiniwin replied as she jammed the rock into the pocket of her jeans.

Reenie hopped off the bed. "Many dollars," she said, pointing to the rocks on the dresser and the nightstands. Then she picked up Tripod, tucked him under her arm, and disappeared down the hall, singing about her poshed kitty.

"Well," said Jiniwin as she picked up her math book, "I guess we've stalled long enough. The decimals await."

We did our math problems and were writing our opinions of a Robert Frost poem for English when Jiniwin said, out of the blue, "I feel like a prisoner."

"What?"

She tossed her hair back. "Locked up in school all day, and then the teachers assign all this extra work for us to do at home. And look at me—I can't even go home to do it, because Paulette's not there yet."

"You, a prisoner? A girl with her own pink telephone? Get real."

"I'd give back the phone and everything else if I could have a normal home like you."

"When pigs fly!"

Jiniwin stretched out on the bed and propped her hand against her cheek. "I mean it. Even when Paulette's home, she's glued to the computer, typing up trial transcripts. Once in a while, I'd like to sit down and have dinner and a conversation with her. But no, I heat up a frozen burrito or a pizza in the microwave and eat all by myself, like a prisoner in a cell."

Reenie came in, smelling of bubble bath and looking soft and cuddly in her baby-doll pajamas. She was carrying Tripod, who was batting at the new ribbon Mom had woven into the neckline of the old pj's.

"You got a new ribbon," I said.

"Wellow," she replied, meaning yellow, her favorite color.

"It'll make you have sweet dreams." I turned down the covers of my sister's bed, and she climbed in with Tripod.

Mom and Dad came in to kiss Reenie good night, and Jiniwin and I transferred our things to the kitchen, where the countertops shone and the electric range sparkled. A cupboard door was open, and I saw the canned food rack Dad had built in the cupboard. I thought of the writing wall in the hallway. My throat stung with sadness. How I would miss this house. It was a Richter family original. Unique.

Jiniwin fished a stray can of sauerkraut out from under the table, placed it in the rack, and watched it rumble down the chute before she shut the cupboard door. "This place won't ever be the same without you guys," she said wistfully.

I figured we'd both be bawling bucketfuls in a minute if I didn't do something. Picking up Groucho, I said, "Oh, yuk."

"What's the matter?"

"He's dirtied his drawers, and we're fresh out of Pampers."

She flashed me a goofy grin. "Remember when we were little, and we were always trying to cheer each other up? Like the day I wet my pants in kindergarten, you let me wear your Best Rester Badge."

"And when my grandma died, you drew me a picture of an angel bathed in sunshine and floating on a cloud."

"What a team!" said Jiniwin, linking arms with me. At the shrill ring of the phone, she pulled me over and picked up the receiver. "Hello? Yeah, it's me. Be there in a minute." Hanging up, she said, "That was a subpoena from Her Honor."

I nodded and fetched Dad. One of my parents' rules was that we girls couldn't go out alone after dark.

Paulette had turned on plenty of lights, illuminating the stained-glass windows at the front door. I'd always felt poor next to Jiniwin. Now, thinking about that horrid farmhouse, I felt like an absolute pauper. For a second, as Jiniwin stood in the doorway, I imagined her surrounded by jewels. My eyes watered, and the colors of the glass melted together in a jumble.

On the way back to our house, Dad held my hand. He hadn't done that in a long time, and his palm felt strangely smooth. "Buddy, I know you'll miss the close contact with Jiniwin, and we'll all miss this nice neighborhood. But we'll be okay at Aunt Ruby's."

I knew he wanted me to tell him I wouldn't mind moving to the country, but that would have been a bald-faced lie, and I'd have choked on it.

When we got home, I showered and went to bed. My mind wandered to Aunt Ruby's farm, back when there were cattle down by the creek and hogs in the barn lot, not in the front yard. I'd played fairy princess under the pink canopy of a tulip tree, and laughed as hummingbirds dipped into the flowers, their tiny wings blurring, going nowhere fast. That had been a long time ago, before I started school, before Reenie learned to walk, before Aunt Ruby had her breakdown, before Dad lost his job.

Now I was in the eighth grade, Reenie ran off every chance she got, Aunt Ruby was dead, and Dad was moving us to that awful place. There'd been no warning, no family discussion, and nobody to care that a thirteen-year-old girl hated having her roots pulled right out of the ground.

Soon I heard the murmur of my parents' voices in the kitchen. Although Mom would normally sleep a couple of hours before going on the midnight shift, tonight she and Dad were talking about getting the utilities hooked up at the farm and borrowing a pickup.

At eleven-fifty, I heard her leaving for work and Dad going to bed. By then, I had my covers all tied up in knots. I tossed them aside, then crept out to the bathroom for a drink. By the night-light in the hall, I saw these words on the writing wall: "Farewell to recess and bossy old Bly. Buddy and Jiniwin are in junior high!"

Our family history. How could Mom bear to leave it all behind?

As I crawled back into my bed, Reenie rolled over in hers and giggled in her sleep. After we moved to the country, she'd be safer. Jim Bob would have his wheels. Mom and Dad would have fewer bills and worries. Still, I wanted to stay in this room, in this house, on this street. This was *home*.

Dad coughed in the other room. I thought about him losing his job and his pride. I thought about losing *my* pride at a ramshackle house with a hog shed attached.

My sleep came in fits and starts. In my dreams, I wore myself out, running back and forth but accomplishing nothing—just going nowhere fast.

FIVE
Last Hurrah

I HELPED REENIE GET DRESSED for school in a plaid jumper and red tights, then went looking for the hairbrush. Whether Mom was home or not, fixing Reenie's hair was my job. For reasons known only to my sister, she'd declare, "Hands off!" if anybody but me touched her head. And once she set her mind on something, there was no changing it.

When she saw the hairbrush, she said, "Pong tails."

"Pony tails take too long."

"Pong tails." She pooched out her lower lip and placed her hands on her hips.

I knew I was whipped, so I fixed the pong tails and tied them with red yarn.

"My s-sissy. My pong tails," Reenie sang as she swished them back and forth and admired herself in the mirror.

While I was getting dressed, she found a red plastic

purse that matched her outfit and chose some rocks to put in it. Then she sat on the bed to wait for me, red purse on one side and the flowered purse on the other.

Dad, Reenie, Jim Bob, and I ate breakfast together. When Dad finished eating, he nodded toward Reenie's purses on Mom's chair, and asked me, "Have you checked for contraband?"

"Not yet, but I will."

Reenie had a fascination for matches, cigarette lighters, candles—anything associated with fire. We'd bought the electric range, even though we couldn't afford it, because Reenie delighted in poking papers and sticks in a flame.

Dad checked the contents of her purses. "All clear. Just one egg and some rocks."

"Dollars, Dod. My dollars." Reenie downed the last of her milk and stood up.

I got up too, and began patting her pockets.

"Against the wall, buster. Spread 'em," growled Jim Bob, like a TV cop.

Feeling a suspicious lump beneath the folds of Reenie's jumper, I reached in and found a disposable cigarette lighter.

"My sister, the firebug," said Jim Bob, and he tweaked one of her pong tails.

"Hands off," she said.

"Reenie, where'd you get that?" asked Dad.

"My fire." She reached for the lighter, but I closed my fingers over it, then passed it over to Dad.

He dropped it into his shirt pocket and shook his

head. "It's not mine. Who knows where she got it? Reenie, how many times have we told you it's dangerous to play with fire?"

In response, she gave him a big, sunshiny smile and a hug.

After that, I tried to talk her into leaving the flowered purse at home. No telling what other kids would say or do when they learned that she had an egg baby. As usual, though, I lost the argument. We girls left the house with me carrying my books and Miss Molly, and Reenie clutching both of her purses in a death grip.

The air was cool and dreary with fog, and because it was trash day, bulging bags and sagging boxes huddled in forlorn piles along the street.

"Yuk. The fragrance of Friday," I said when we caught a whiff of something rotten.

"Yeah, s-sissy."

At Jiniwin's house, the porch was empty, except for two metal lawn chairs and a plant stand bursting with lavender chrysanthemums.

"Jivven?" asked Reenie.

"Must be running late. She'll be out in a minute."

Reenie clambered up the steps and had her hand on the doorknob when I said, "Let's not go in. It'll slow her down. Let's just sit and wait."

We sat on the cold, damp steps and hunkered down inside our jackets.

After a couple of minutes, the door burst open and

Jiniwin came out apologizing. "Sorry. Couldn't get it all together this morning."

"Hi, Jivven," said Reenie as she and I stood up.

"Hi." In Jiniwin's arms were her schoolbooks, a paper sack, and Groucho. She dumped everything on a chair and used both hands to fit her key in the lock. When she turned around, I saw that her eyes were red.

"Have you and Paulette been fighting again?" I asked.

"No, she's not even home. It's that moving business. Couldn't sleep, and got up with a headache," said Jiniwin, picking up her things and sailing past us off the porch.

I grabbed Reenie's hand and hurried to catch up. "You look like you've been crying."

"I got soap in my eyes when I washed my hair. Made me blind for thirty minutes." Turning her bloodshot gaze on Reenie, Jiniwin changed the subject. "I see you're carrying two purses this morning."

"My baby. My dollars," replied Reenie.

As we left the subdivision and started up Gorrell toward Main, I asked Jiniwin, "Is that your lunch in the sack? Did you forget this is pizza day?"

"Ugh. Don't talk about food this early, or I'll upchuck."

"It never bothered you before."

"Well, it's bothering me now."

Upset stomach again, and her breath had a sour-fruit smell. Maybe it was nerves, or a virus. "So what's in the sack?" I asked.

"A trashy novel."

"Since when did you start reading trashy novels?"

"I didn't. I found it in the john, and I'm gonna pitch it somewhere. Hey, Reenie, how is Rosebud this morning?"

Reenie patted the flowered purse. "My baby."

"All cracked up about going to school," I said, and Jiniwin grinned for the first time since coming out to meet us.

By now, I had the distinct impression that she was hiding something, but I kept my mouth shut. She knew I was willing to listen, and she'd confide in me when she was ready.

"There's that Dallas guy again," said Jiniwin, her voice laced with disapproval.

Ahead of us, Dallas Benge was performing his Friday-morning ritual of sorting through other people's trash to find items to sell at the flea market. He pulled out a footstool and a picture frame and laid them in a cart tied behind his bike.

Kids around town called Dallas an eccentric, a ragpicker, a pack rat, but he wasn't some old bum who hopped freight cars. He was a sophomore, an honor student at Turnback Junior-Senior High School. He wasn't much to look at—tall and skinny with jug-handle ears, clothes always faded and wrinkled, straight brown hair a bit shaggy. Still, he'd caught my attention, simply because he'd taken a liking to Reenie.

"My boy," she announced as she pulled me along toward him.

Dallas often gave her some little present he'd found—a pencil box, a plastic windmill, a toy car minus a wheel. It embarrassed me for him to give her castoffs right here in the street, but I could live with it. I wondered what kind of home life Dallas had, what kind of parents would allow him to scavenge in the trash.

A carful of high school boys drove by slowly, and we heard taunts and laughter:

"Whatcha doin', Benge? Christmas shopping?"

"Naw, he's makin' money."

"Has to. His old man's always on a binge."

I frowned. Mr. Benge on a "binge"? Was that a fact or just a cruel play on words?

Dallas ignored the boys and concentrated on fitting a beat-up suitcase and a toaster into the cart. When he saw us girls approaching, he said, "Good morning," and his big ears turned red. I figured he had a crush on Jiniwin, like just about every other boy in Turnback.

She breezed past him with a nod.

"Hi, boy," said Reenie, stopping dead in her tracks. Of course, I stopped, too.

"Hi, Reenie. Got a present for you."

"Goody, goody," she replied, and clapped her hands with glee.

I glanced around quickly, hoping no one was watching. I couldn't see anyone but Jiniwin, who was replacing the lid on a trash can a couple of driveways down.

Dallas was eyeing her, even as he handed Reenie an evening purse with sequins missing and threads hanging.

"Oh, boy!" said Reenie, plopping her red purse onto my stack of books and snatching up the shiny one.

"Shouldn't you keep that to sell?" I asked. If Mr. Benge really was a drinker, Dallas probably needed every dime he could get his hands on.

He forced his attention back to me. "What? Oh, it wouldn't bring much with those beads missing. Besides, a guy likes to give his best girl a present once in a while. Right, Reenie?"

"Yeah, boy."

Indicating Miss Molly's basket, Dallas asked, "Is that an egg?"

"It used to be. Now it's a baby for a family living project."

"Sounds interesting." Taking hold of his bike, he started rolling it to the next driveway. "Don't mean to be rude," he said, "but I have to keep moving so I'll finish on Main in time for the ten-minute bell. The janitor locks my cart in his storage shed, and I'm in my seat in algebra class while the other kids are still looking for their books."

"Bet you're the teacher's pet," I said as Reenie and I crowded in beside him on the sidewalk.

Dallas laughed out loud. "Not exactly. Mrs. Foster steers clear of me, especially on Fridays. A ragpicker might have cooties, you know."

I stared at him. How could he call himself a ragpicker and just brush it off?

"Don't look so shocked, Buddy. I know what people think of me, but it doesn't matter. What matters is what I think of myself."

His words were still ringing in my head when Reenie and I caught up with Jiniwin.

She tossed a lock of hair back over her shoulder, and said, "I don't know why you want to talk to a guy whose high point of the week is trash day. He gives me the willies. He smells like dirt and mustard."

"How would you know that?" I asked, feeling a strange need to defend Dallas. "You don't get close enough to smell him."

"I've heard it from other kids," she said, as if that made it gospel. "They say he eats mustard sandwiches for lunch."

"*They say?* Other kids are cruel. You know that. Look how some of them treat Reenie."

"Okay, okay. I just think he's an oddball, always selling that junk at the flea market."

"Oddball or not, he's good to Reenie, and that's more than I can say about half the population of Turnback."

◆ ◆ ◆

Groucho and Miss Molly made a hit at school. Hordes of kids huddled around Jiniwin and me to admire our artistic abilities. I'd been dying to get Lonnie Joe Ross's attention for weeks, when all I had to do was put hair and a nose on an egg, and he stood up and took notice.

"Hey, Buddy, that's pretty cool," he said, picking up the egg basket I'd set on the floor so I could unload my books in my locker.

I buried Reenie's red purse under the books before answering him. "Thanks," I said, focusing on the lock of curly black hair that had fallen across his forehead. I wanted to keep the conversation going, impress him with my wit or something, but I couldn't think of another word to say. Why was it I could talk to Dallas Benge easily, but was tongue-tied when it came to Lonnie Joe Ross?

In English third hour, Mr. Pettigrew broke up laughing about our eggs. He was in such a good mood after that, he collected the papers we'd written about the Robert Frost poem instead of having us read them aloud. What a relief. Being chubby makes you nervous about standing in front of a class.

Fifth hour, in family living, I halfway expected Mrs. Blatterman to be mad about what we'd done to our eggs. Instead, she held up Groucho and Miss Molly for everyone to see. "Jiniwin and Buddy are to be commended for personalizing their babies," she said. "It shows they're taking parenting seriously."

How she could think those homely faces were "serious" was beyond me, but I didn't argue the point.

Seventh hour, Jiniwin and I walked together to science class. We could see our teacher, Mrs. Royal, standing under the banner in the doorway: FREE KNOWLEDGE. BRING YOUR OWN CONTAINER. She was joking with students as they entered the classroom, revving them up after a long, hard day.

Mrs. Royal was short and dumpy with mousy brown hair, and her most distinguishing characteristic was the mole above the nosepiece of her glasses. She was a terrific teacher, though, and her class was my favorite, except on Fridays, when we had to work with the animals in the living lab.

As Jiniwin and I passed by her, she peeked at Groucho and Miss Molly and chuckled. "Fortunately, they don't resemble their mothers."

After taking roll, she beamed at Gary Simmons. "Gary, that high F on your test, averaged in with your lab grade, makes you this week's most improved student. You may lead your team to the lab. Other teams, fall in behind."

We traipsed down the hall to the lab, where creatures were waiting to eat or be eaten. The bubbling aquarium contained the goldfish that were the main course of Jaws, the foot-long alligator. A glass cage teemed with crickets that would be doled out to Harry, the tarantula. Two dozen baby white mice scampered and squeaked in their cage, unaware that they were on the menu for Jake, the baby boa constrictor.

Other cages held Goomer the iguana, a fire-bellied toad, a hermit crab, salamanders, frogs, a guinea pig, and an Egyptian mouse.

I listened carefully for Team Three's assignment. If we had to feed today, I wanted the mammals. They ate hamster pellets—no squishing or bleeding when chomped.

"Team Four, clean the cages," said Mrs. Royal. "Team One, measure the animals and report to Team Two, who will update the growth charts. Team Three, do the feeding."

"I'll feed Precious and Porky," I said quickly, choosing the guinea pig and the Egyptian mouse.

"I'll take Jake," said Jiniwin. She was already checking the wall chart to see how many mice to feed the baby boa.

The thought made me queasy. I'd watched Jake eat only once. The tiny mouse, swallowed whole, had made a major lump in his throat. As Jiniwin reached into the mice's cage to catch Jake's dinner, I turned away, measured out the hamster pellets for Precious and Porky, and poured them into the feeding trays.

Porky munched contentedly on the pellets. I stared at his body, prickly as a hedgehog but soft to the touch, and thought about what I'd say to him if Mrs. Royal ever sent me in to talk. Would I tell him I didn't want to move to a tumbledown house in the country?

That I didn't want to be close neighbors to reptiles and varmints? What a laugh. I'd get no sympathy from Porky, who lived between an alligator and a snake.

When Jiniwin and I picked Reenie up after school, she took one look at Groucho and Miss Molly and showed us that her flowered purse was empty, except for some bits of shell and egg yolk. "Gone," she said.

"She sat on it, accidentally," explained Mrs. Houston. "That was the end of the egg baby."

"Did she cry?" I asked.

"No. We traded—my cupcake for her scrambled egg."

Jiniwin offered her egg basket to Reenie. "You want to carry Groucho?"

"Too haiby."

"It's not too heavy."

"Too haiby," repeated my sister. With a shake of her pong tails, she marched down the steps.

"I guess she's tired of eggs," I said as Jiniwin and I followed her.

Jiniwin tossed her hair back. "So am I. And I sure don't want to take Groucho to the skating contest this weekend."

"What skating contest?"

"Sunday afternoon at the Rainbow Rink. For a dollar, we can skate as long as we want. Whoever lasts the longest gets a free pass for a year. Lonnie Joe just told me about it as we were cleaning up the lab. You know, Buddy, this could be your big chance to catch his eye."

"Huh?"

"Think about it. In that dark rink with the glittering disco lights and the throbbing music, he can't help but notice how graceful you are on skates. You're absolutely weightless, in fact."

I grinned at her, and the grin stayed with me all the way home. That contest would be my fabulous farewell to Turnback. It would be my last hurrah.

SIX

The Witch's Head

IN MY DREAM, Jaws was not a twelve-inch alligator, but a dinosaur straight out of *Jurassic Park*. When he opened his mouth to bite me, I came up swinging and nearly flung myself out of bed.

The phone was ringing. It was still dark outside, and I flopped back down and snuggled up under my covers with a groan. Only one person would call that early on Saturday morning—Aunt Sage, our sweet old neighbor, who didn't seem nearly as sweet at this moment.

"Buddy," said Mom, touching my shoulder, "Aunt Sage's paper landed in the bushes this morning. Would you run over and get it?"

"Mnghhh."

"Now, please. You know how she is when she wants something. She's liable to get a ladder and go after it herself. Old people's bones get brittle, and if she fell, she could easily break a hip."

"For crying out loud, Mom. The world won't stop turning if she has to wait for the paper."

"She won't wait. She'll get it one way or another. Come on. Get up. It's time to rise and shine, anyway. We've got to work at the farm."

I dragged myself out of bed and threw on a pair of jeans, an old sweatshirt, and sneakers, then headed up the street toward the only house on the block with a porch light burning.

The door opened, and there stood Aunt Sage, who at eighty-four resembled a scarecrow in the light. Wispy hairs had escaped from her nighttime braids, and the legs beneath her nightgown looked like Popsicle sticks. She was dragging something out the door, and when she started bumping it down the steps, I saw it was a folding ladder.

Instantly alert, I sprinted across the lawn. "Here," I said, "let me do that." I positioned the ladder, climbed up, and fetched the paper from the flowering almond bush by the porch.

"Buddy, you're a sweetheart. I'm sorry I had to wake you."

"It's okay. I had to get up early anyway. We're going out to the farm." As soon as the words were out, I wanted to bite my tongue. It wasn't a farm. Not anymore. It was a dump.

"My, that brings back memories," said Aunt Sage, retying the strings of the bed jacket she'd crocheted herself. "Did I ever tell you about the dairy farm Herbert and I operated in Pettis County? He was born in that house. The story goes that he fell down the steps as a toddler and rolled out to the barn, and stayed there his whole life. . . ."

The sun had been up for a while before I could get back to the house. By then, I'd had two cups of spiced tea, three slices of cinnamon toast, and an earful of cow stories. Not once had Aunt Sage glanced at the newspaper.

Mom was packing a picnic lunch. Dad was brewing up some cream of wheat, instead of our usual Saturday breakfast of sausage and pancakes.

"None for me," I said. "I had cinnamon toast at Aunt Sage's."

In our room, Reenie greeted me by asking for pong tails. I fixed them and reached for some blue ribbons.

"Wellow," she said.

"The blue matches your eyes."

"Wellow."

She won, of course. A minute later, sporting her yellow ribbons, she bounced off to the kitchen for breakfast.

As I ran the brush through my wiry mop, I frowned at my reflection in the mirror and decided to change the sweatshirt. It flattened my chest and emphasized my spare tire.

"Square body—just like a milk carton," said Jim Bob from the doorway.

I whirled around. "Don't you believe in knocking? Nobody can have any privacy in this house!"

"Try the refrigerator. The other milk cartons like it."

"Get out!" I threw the hairbrush, and it crashed against the slamming door.

The door opened again almost immediately, but it wasn't Jim Bob standing there. It was Mom. She bent over and picked up the hairbrush, and I expected a chewing out. "Jim Bob's mouth is working this morning," she said as she tossed me the brush. "Let's hope the rest of him can do the same."

I caught the brush and gave her a grin.

"You'd better call Jiniwin," she said. "Make sure she's up and ready."

"Soon as I change my shirt." I went to my parents' room and put on one of Dad's chambray shirts. He never minded my doing that, as long as he had a clean one when he needed it. On me, the shirts were big and sloppy and comfortable.

As I left the room, I almost fell over Jim Bob, who was squatted down in the hall, tying his sneakers.

"Ella, the farm girl," he said, looking me up and down. "All you need is a John Deere cap and a pair of overalls."

I stuck my tongue out at him and went to the phone in the kitchen, but instead of a dial tone, I heard yammering from Aunt Sage's TV. "Tell me, Mom," I said, "how can Aunt Sage remember a five-legged calf born forty years ago, yet forget to hang up the phone?"

"Old age, hon. I see it every day at the nursing home. Run over and hang up her receiver, then go see about Jiniwin. We'll pick you girls up in a few minutes."

I fetched Miss Molly, slipped over to Aunt Sage's and hung up the phone without her knowing I was there, then went to Jiniwin's.

"Tent shirt again, huh?" she said as she let me in. She looked slim and trim in Calvin Klein jeans and a pink Oxford shirt, and her hair was pulled back low on her neck with a barrette.

"Hey, the possums and squirrels wouldn't care if I wore a *real* tent."

"You're hopeless." Her eyes were red, as if she'd been up half the night staring at the tube.

"How can you do that?" I asked, thinking out loud.

"Do what?"

"Watch the 'Late Show.' After the ten o'clock news, I get deathly sleepy."

"Don't I know it? Your snores drown out the television."

I grinned and followed her into that beautiful blue living room, where cartoons were playing on TV.

"Coke and potato chips for breakfast?" I said, eyeing the food on the coffee table.

"Paulette's sleeping in, and it's too much trouble to cook just for myself."

"Oh." I couldn't understand Paulette. She was gone at least three nights a week, and most mornings when Jiniwin got out of bed. You'd think she'd at least want to eat with her daughter on weekends.

Jiniwin frowned in the direction of Paulette's bedroom. "Her Honor doesn't like to be seen in the mornings, anyway, before she's applied all the goop and the eye paint and dolled herself up like a floozy."

A floozy? My eyes popped. That was a pretty strong word to describe your mother.

"It's true," Jiniwin said. "When Frank was around, she didn't use makeup at all, and she looked great. Now she looks cheap."

"So that's why you don't wear the stuff. I thought you were worried about zits."

The front door opened, and my sister walked in.

"Reenie," I said, "you're supposed to knock."

"Yeah-kay." She grinned and stuck her thumb in her mouth. "Hi, Jivven."

"Hi, Reenie. You're not going to eat off that nail polish, are you?"

"Yeah, girl." She ambled over, sat down beside Jiniwin, and stared at the cartoons.

Soon Jiniwin and I went down the hall, so she could brush her teeth and pick up Groucho. As I walked into the cotton candy atmosphere of her bedroom, I said, "It smells different in here."

Jiniwin waved a hand toward a clear glass bowl on the dresser. "It must be my strawberry potpourri."

"It's more like that bottle of stuff Reenie broke the

other day. You know—kind of fruity, but not strawberries."

"Probably because it's artificial," she said from her bathroom.

I sniffed the air, certain that I wasn't smelling anything close to strawberry potpourri. "It's wine. Has Paulette been in here this morning?"

"No. I told you she won't let me see her until she gets all painted up."

"Have you had wine in here for some reason?"

"What is this? An inquisition?" Jiniwin asked, her voice edged with irritation.

"No. I'm just curious. To lighten her mood, I said, "Hey, I know what it is."

She stuck her head in the doorway and said "What?" around a mouthful of toothpaste.

I cut my eyes to the poster. "It's that pumpkin rotting."

Jiniwin giggled. "Buddy Richter, you're wacky. You know that?"

"I know. I got it from Aunt Ruby."

When we returned to the living room, Reenie was gone. Through the window, I saw our station wagon stopping down the street, and her climbing in with a bag under her arm. "Reenie's got your potato chips," I said.

"But she left me a dollar," replied Jiniwin, pointing at a rock on the coffee table. "I'd say that's a pretty fair trade."

Dad honked, and we took our eggs outside. The

rear of the wagon was crammed full—cooler, mops, brooms, scrub bucket, cleaning supplies, tools, lawn-mower.

"This looks like the 'Beverly Hillbillies,' " Jiniwin said as she climbed into the backseat next to Jim Bob. I scrunched in beside her, glad to have the window instead of the hump.

The car started rolling, and Jim Bob laid his arm across the back of the seat. "Bzzzt!" he said, and poked at my ear with his finger.

I slapped his hand away, but I kept my mouth shut. Sometimes the best way to deal with a pest is to ignore him.

"Fair warning," said Mom, turning in her seat to address Jiniwin. "After Aunt Ruby came back to Missouri, she developed an obsession for collecting things, maybe because she saw so much deprivation in other countries. Anyway, she gathered up an awful assortment of junk, and you're going to see it today."

"I thought you sold all her stuff to pay for the funeral," Jim Bob said.

Dad shook his head. "Just the furniture. Nobody would have wanted all that other conglomeration. Balls of string, old food in jars, buttons, postcards, newspapers, just boxes and boxes of junk that weren't of use to her or anybody else."

"Oh, she found a use for some of it," said Mom. "Remember the year she gave us that homemade chandelier for our anniversary? It was a bunch of egg cartons glued together, with holes poked in the egg cups."

"I remember," said Dad, nodding. "I saved it until she died, and I still feel guilty about throwing it away."

"Well, you shouldn't," Mom said. "Those last few months, she wasn't rational. If she was, she wouldn't have built that hog shed onto the house."

"What happened to her?" asked Jiniwin. "Did she have old-timer's disease?"

Mom chuckled. "It's called Alzheimer's disease, but no, that wasn't her problem. Alzheimer's comes on slowly, whereas Aunt Ruby changed all at once. We think she had a stroke, but she wouldn't let James put her in the nursing home. We came out to check on her every weekend, and we paid a neighbor lady to bring her hot meals."

I hadn't known about the meals. "A neighbor lady?"

"Wilma Benge," replied Mom.

"Is that Dallas's mother?"

"I don't know," Mom said. "I talked to her on the phone a few times, but only about Aunt Ruby."

"Bzzzt!" That pesky Jim Bob poked my ear again. Still determined to ignore him, I gazed out the window.

We were passing the fairgrounds, where the flea market was in full swing. People were milling about, looking at used furniture, dishes, tires, and tools. I couldn't see Dallas, but I knew he'd be there somewhere, hawking the footstool, the suitcase, the toaster and whatever else he'd salvaged from yesterday's trash.

A mile beyond the fairgrounds, Dad turned off the highway onto a secondary blacktop, and I started watching for the old brick silo that would mark our next turnoff. I hadn't been out this way for a long time, but that silo had always fascinated me because it had a tree growing out of it.

Dad slowed down to make the turn, and I spied the silo. Branches with green-and-gold leaves were spilling right out its top.

"That can't be a real tree," said Jiniwin as Dad steered onto a gravel road. She sneezed at the dust sifting into the car, then asked, "How can it grow there?"

"Fluke of nature," Dad said. "A bird dropped a seed, the seed sprouted, and the sprout just kept reaching for the sun. It was determined to grow, in spite of the obstacles along the way."

"Like my Humpty Dumpty baby," said Mom, smiling at Reenie.

"You mean the Flash," said Jim Bob, and he leaned over the seat and tweaked one of Reenie's pong tails.

She hunched up her shoulders. "Hands off."

"He can't keep his hands off anybody," I said. "He's like an octopus back here." When he buzzed my ear again, I shot him a hateful look and warned, "Do that one more time and I'll bite off that finger."

Mom turned around and leveled a glance at Jim Bob. "Son, either act your age, or lose your driver's license."

That knocked the wind out of his sails. Nothing was more important to my brother than his driver's license.

When he quit pestering me, I settled back and concentrated on the scenery. Cows chewing, cows mooing, cows lifting their tails and watering flat rocks. I winced, recalling the time one of Aunt Ruby's cows had splattered me with green manure.

"Almost there," Dad said, bringing me back to the present. He was turning off the first gravel road onto another that cut a path between endless trees and barbed-wire fences. The green and gold and red of every leaf, every weed, was muted with dust. Desolate. Boring.

" 'Benge,' " said Jiniwin, reading the name on a rusty mailbox. "Is that the neighbor who cooked for Aunt Ruby?"

"That's the one," replied Dad.

Still wondering if Wilma Benge might be Dallas's mother, I gazed up the driveway. It curved back behind some trees, so I couldn't see a house.

A little farther on, Dad pointed out a giant mossy mound in the woods and told Jiniwin, "That's a clay pit—one of many around these parts. Years ago, they used the clay to make pottery."

The pit meant we were almost to Aunt Ruby's. I drew a deep breath and stared out the windshield.

The road curved to the left, but Aunt Ruby's private lane lay straight ahead. There was her house, sitting in the middle of a field of weeds and back-lighted by the sun.

The house was even worse than I remembered. Time and neglect had turned it into a weathered-gray witch's head. The peaked roof was her pointed hat, and the sagging left side of the porch was a brim pulled down over one eye. The tarpapered shed was a wart on her chin. Even the tulip tree where I'd played fairy princess was as ratty as a witch's broom, and the blooms were gone. Why was it that the things you liked could never stay the same?

We entered the drive over a trestle of railroad ties that served as a cattle guard—and hit such a bump that Dad's head thunked against the top of the car. At that instant, the sun was visible through the house's front door window, and the oval glass lit up like a burning eye.

"That cattle guard's a real brain-scrambler," Dad said, rubbing his head as we bounced along the rutted lane.

"And that hog shed's a real eyesore," said Mom. "Jim Bob, first thing, I want you to tear down the shed and the fence wire and shovel out the manure."

"Ah, Mom—" he began, but Reenie said, "Pretty birds," and pointed.

All eyes turned to the pond at our right, where half a dozen mallard ducks were swimming peacefully, leaving tiny wakes in the clear water.

Catching Reenie's outstretched finger, Mom cautioned her, "You must *never* go to the pond by yourself."

"She'll be okay, Irene," said Dad. "The pond's got a fence around it, except for that little bit close to the road, and that part's only knee deep."

"Still, I don't want her going there by herself. There could be snakes."

The instant she said that, I started scoping out the yard. A snake in a cage at school was bad enough. Out here, I'd have to watch every step. I breathed a little easier when I saw Dad was pulling up near the gravel walkway, where there weren't any weeds to hide snakes.

The big chunks of quartz lining the walkway winked in the sunlight, and Reenie cried, "Many dollars!" As soon as the car stopped rolling, she crawled over Mom and bailed out.

"I'm gonna take a gander at the pickup," said Jim Bob, heading off in the direction of the barn.

I couldn't resist a jeer. "Bring back a shovel for hog poop."

He turned and touched his forehead in a mocking salute. "Sure thing, Ella."

Dad unlocked the front door, then came back to help unload the station wagon. Jiniwin and I, carrying our eggs and the mops and brooms, were the first ones to enter the house.

It smelled of age and mothballs and dampness. Heavy, ragged curtains made the living room too dark. When Jiniwin flipped a switch, an egg carton chandelier shrouded with cobwebs sent out little circles of light.

Although the room ran the whole length of the house, its only stick of furniture was an upright piano covered with dust and mouse tracks. Cardboard boxes, like forgotten tombstones, littered the scuffed and dirty hardwood floor. Chewed postcards and other papers were strewn everywhere.

"It's definitely not a dude ranch," Jiniwin said, her voice sounding hollow in the emptiness.

My body flushed hot with shame.

The piano tinkled, and we turned in time to see a mouse leap off the keys and scramble underneath it. "Tripod's gonna love it here," Jiniwin said.

"Reenie, too—as soon as she discovers the piano." At church, I had to escort my sister to and from her Sunday school class to keep her away from the piano in the basement. Otherwise, kids would egg her on to play it, then make fun of her when she did. She couldn't really play, of course, but she pounded at the keys for all she was worth.

We opened a window, deposited our babies on the sill, then looked around downstairs, setting off bombardments of dust particles in every shaft of sunlight. The more I saw, the worse I felt. Dining room, bathroom, sewing room—all were cluttered with egg cartons, newspapers, boxes, and fruit jars containing murky liquid.

In the kitchen, the range top was speckled with

mouse droppings, the ceiling fixture was black with dead bugs, and the cabinets were dull with ancient varnish. A potbellied stove and a wood box in the corner no doubt meant we'd be heating with wood.

Off the kitchen was a narrow, dark stairway. We climbed it and checked out the rooms upstairs, where the ceilings slanted like drooping shoulders.

Four bedrooms. I could have a room of my own, but I didn't want that. Reenie and I'd roomed together her whole life. I liked feeling protective, and she liked having her sissy close by.

Knowing me as well as she did, Jiniwin had already figured that out. We were standing in a room with a window seat in the corner when she asked, "Which room you gonna pick for you and Reenie?"

"This one," I said, frowning at an Africa-shaped stain, which started at the ceiling and trailed across the brown roses of the wallpaper. "If I could like anything in this house, I'd like reading on that window seat." I walked over and looked at the view—backyard in one direction, barn lot in the other.

A discordant sound drifted up from downstairs, and I knew Reenie had found the piano. She started banging on the keys and singing about "the farm," "pretty birdies," and "many dollars."

I walked over and lifted the lid of the window seat, then dropped it with a yelp as a mouse jumped onto my foot and skittered across the floor.

Jiniwin squealed, and she and the mouse hot-footed it around each other. When the mouse escaped into the hallway, she cautiously opened the window seat.

It was crammed full of junk. On top of the heap were a shoe box containing rusty nails and bolts and washers, and a cigar box containing buttons and bottle caps.

Jiniwin picked up a washer and idly slipped it on her finger. "Buddy, I know your Aunt Ruby was bonkers, but I kind of understand her collecting. Remember back when everything I found was a 'treasure'—a marble, a bird's egg, a rock with a hole in it? Paulette used to scold me and throw the stuff away. I got to where I'd sneak things into my room and hide them in a cigar box in my cedar chest."

I remembered. Jiniwin had made a necklace of the rock with the hole in it, believing it was a good-luck charm that would bring her parents back together. After Paulette found out, she wouldn't let her wear it.

Jiniwin went on, turning the washer around and around on her finger, "Paulette thinks if it's not worth a bundle and in a flashy package, it's not worth keeping. She dumped Frank. Said she was tired of being married to a grease monkey. It wasn't any time before she had that fancy lawyer on the string."

It was hard to sympathize, considering that my problems at the moment seemed a whole lot worse than hers. Instead of saying something that might make her mad, I just stood listening to the waves of Reenie's "music" crashing through the house.

"I feel so lonely sometimes," Jiniwin said. "I miss my dad, but I don't think he misses me."

I heaved a sigh. "I guess we're a long ways from the days when a Best Rester Badge and an angel drawing can make things right again."

Jiniwin kept on twisting the washer. "Buddy, if I tell you something, will you promise—" A shadow fell across the doorway, and she looked up sharply and stopped talking.

Mom, her arms folded, stood there tapping her foot in irritation. "While you girls are loafing," she snapped, "the mold is multiplying downstairs."

"Sorry, Mom. We'll be down in a minute."

"I'm counting on that," she said, and left.

"What were you fixing to tell me?" I asked Jiniwin.

"Nothing." She tossed the washer back into the window seat, and rubbed that spot on her finger. "It was nothing, really. Forget I brought it up."

I was curious about what was going on in her head, but not really worried. With her flair for melodrama, even a broken fingernail could be a catastrophe.

When we got downstairs, Mom shouted over the music, "Girls, sweep a path from the living room to the back door. If we don't move that piano to the barn, we'll all be deaf by noon."

We cleared a path, but the piano got moved only as far as the backyard. It was too heavy to lift, and its wheels would barely roll. With all of us shoving, we managed to push it up against the base of a tree so close to the porch that branches were brushing the roof.

"This'll have to do for now," Dad wheezed.

"Someday we'll get some more manpower out here and move this beast out of the weather."

Thirty seconds later, Reenie was banging away under the shade tree, broadcasting her music to the whole outdoors. It wasn't so bad with a couple of walls between us, and as long as we could hear it, we didn't have to wonder where she was.

SEVEN

The Snake Catcher

"MIGHT AS WELL START at the front and work back," Mom said, as she surveyed the living room. "Get rid of the junk in the whole house before we start scrubbing. We'll go through boxes and sort out anything that can be recycled."

"Too bad we don't have a bulldozer," I muttered.

Mom, her face streaked with dirt from the piano, gave me a tired look. "Buddy, if you tackle this job with an attitude, you're going to make yourself and all the rest of us miserable. Is that what you want?"

I shook my head. What I *wanted* was to leave this place and never come back.

Mom climbed onto a box to disassemble the egg carton chandelier. Jiniwin knelt down beside a basket of old shoes and started pawing through it, saying, "Eenie-meenie-miney-mo. Let's see how much of this has to go." With her pink shirt already grimy and a cobweb stuck to her hair, she reminded me of Cinderella scrubbing the hearth. Whatever had been bothering her upstairs seemed to have been forgotten, because she was really going after those shoes.

As I rummaged through a box, I coughed from the mothball smell I was stirring up. A mass of string, wire, rubber bands, and paper clips was tangled up with some woolen coats. Underneath was a handful of stray buttons. I let everything fall back into place, then nudged the box out of the way with my foot.

"What's so special about Texas grapefruit?" asked Jiniwin.

I stared at her.

"That box—it says 'Texas Grapefruit.' I just wondered what makes Texas grapefruit different from Florida's."

"Who knows?" I lowered my voice so Mom wouldn't hear, and added, "Who cares?"

We giggled, as if we had a marvelous secret.

After we'd worked our way through a couple more rooms, I went back to the living room to check on Groucho and Miss Molly. They were still safe on the windowsill, the dingy curtains dancing over them like tattered ghosts. I stood still for a minute, listening to the noises coming in from outside. Wood splintered and nails screeched as Jim Bob ripped at the hog shed. The mower alternately roared and spluttered as Dad tried to cut the weeds. Reenie sang loud enough to be heard in the next county.

I smiled to myself. Those cows were getting the concert of their lives.

"A ray of pure sunshine," Mom said, startling me.

"What?"

"Reenie." Mom brushed a wisp of hair off her forehead. "She's such a happy little girl, it makes me happy just to hear her. I was depressed when we left Turnback this morning, but her serenade is cheering me up."

We came across some copper wire and aluminum that would bring a few dollars at the recycling plant, plus a couple of items we set aside for Reenie—critters painted on pecan shells and an Easter basket made of a big plastic jug.

Mostly, though, our sorting turned up nothing more than dust and junk and cobwebs. Sooner than I had expected, we'd gone through all the boxes downstairs and had stacks of them ready to be hauled outside. Mom sent us girls out to ask Dad where to dump them.

Jim Bob was still hacking away at the hog shed, his blond hair dark with sweat, his wet shirt stuck to his back.

I kicked at a pile of old lumber and picked up a section of two-by-four. "Snake stick," I said to Jiniwin.

"She won't need it," said Jim Bob. "When Ella-Short-for-Elephant makes the ground tremble, they'll run away screaming."

Fury froze my vocal cords, and I couldn't even squawk. My fingers itched to whack him over the head with that two-by-four. At last, I flung it back onto the pile and stomped away, mad enough to kill a dozen snakes with my bare hands.

"Don't listen to him," said Jiniwin, hurrying to catch up. "You know he just does that because you overreact."

I stared at the ground and kept walking.

Dad's lawnmower had stalled out so many times in the weeds, he'd resorted to swinging a hand sickle. He was mopping sweat with a handkerchief when Jiniwin and I asked him about the trash.

"Trash is the least of my worries right now," he grumbled. "Just pile it on those boards in the barn lot. I'll burn it someday when it's not windy."

We were heading back to the house when Jiniwin said, "This place is doing something weird to you guys."

"Huh?"

"You, your mom, your dad, and Jim Bob—you're all acting weird. Maybe this place has cast a spell. You're not yourselves at all."

I told her about the house resembling a witch's head. She couldn't see it, being so close, but she was all for running down to the cattle guard for a look.

"Not now," I said. "Mom'll think we're goofing off. But take my word for it. It's a witch's head."

"Do you think the house is haunted?" she asked, her voice low and confidential. Total melodrama. "Maybe Aunt Ruby's ghost is breathing down your necks because you're throwing away her treasures."

I'd never believed in ghosts, and I sure didn't want to start now. Besides, my parents would kill me if they got wind of such talk. Immediately, I started backtracking. "Haunted, no—not with ghosts and ghouls. It's just a feeling I have about the place. No matter how much work we do around here, it'll never be a real home, and well—it's depressing. To all of us."

"Except to Reenie," said Jiniwin, because we could hear my sister singing her heart out in the backyard.

We went inside, gathered up a load of boxes, and carried them out the back door. When Reenie saw us, she banged on the piano harder and sang louder. Like a true performer, she was playing to her audience.

Every time we passed her with some boxes, she increased her volume for our benefit. Eventually, though, she wandered over to the trash pile and began filling her pockets with buttons.

I pointed out the boards Jim Bob had just added to the pile and told her to watch for nails.

"Yeah-kay." Her gruff voice was lower than usual. She'd sung herself hoarse.

"And don't wander off," I said, handing her a button molded in the shape of a boy and girl.

She smiled at it and dropped it into her pocket. "Yeah-kay, s-sissy. My buttons."

Something told me that I should check those pockets. I did, and turned up two matchbooks with their matches stuck together. They'd drawn dampness and would probably never light, but you just can't take a chance with a firebug. "Reenie Richter," I said, shaking the contraband at her, "you know you're not supposed to play with these. Someday you could hurt yourself real bad."

"My fire," she said, making a grab for the matches.

I held them out of her reach. "Look, Reenie, I'll give in to you on a lot of things, but you *cannot* play with fire."

Pooching out that lower lip, she stuck her hands on her hips.

"Go ahead and pout," I said. "I'd rather see you mad than burned to a crisp."

Later, in an upstairs closet, Mom uncovered an object resembling a fuzzy scarecrow with five sets each of arms and legs. With a grunt, she tossed it into a box of throwaways.

"Is that a Christmas tree?" I asked, retrieving it.

Mom grimaced. "Homemade."

The tree looked primitive, ugly. It stood about two feet tall and was mounted on a round piece of wood painted white and spattered with gold. Its rigid branches were covered with dark-green feathers—the quill parts wrapped so tightly that the feathery parts stuck out all stiff and scraggly.

However, when Reenie saw it on the trash pile, she laid claim to it right away. "S-Santa Claus! Christmas! My tree, s-s-sissy?"

"Maybe," I teased. "Give me a dollar."

"No dollar." She reached into her pocket, pulled out another book of matches, and traded them for the tree.

By lunchtime, we'd all made headway. Aunt Ruby's junk and her hog shed lay in a mountainous heap in the barn lot. The front yard was cleared, the weeds raked into a stack.

Mom laid out our food on the tailgate of the station wagon, and we filled our plates and sat down on a blanket. After Dad asked the blessing, hardly anyone said a word as we devoured salami sandwiches, deviled eggs, and carrot sticks.

Reenie, normally a slow and picky eater, asked for another "sammage" and more "debbled aigs."

Laughing, Mom stood up to oblige. "This country air has done wonders for her appetite. She'll probably turn into a butterball when we move to the farm."

Reenie chomped off the end of a carrot stick. "My farm."

When our bellies were full, the talking began, and I never heard so many plans in my life. Plans for sprucing up the house. For getting a phone hooked up. For filling the propane tank. For planting flower beds. For repairing the pickup.

Even Jiniwin had plans. "James," she said to Dad, "if Paulette would let me buy a horse, could I board it out here?"

Jealousy niggled at me. A horse was the one thing that Jiniwin had wanted forever and hadn't bought.

Dad nodded. "In the spring? I don't see why not. I'll be mending the fence, so I can rent out the pasture for cows."

Jiniwin's eyes got all dreamy. "I'll have to take riding lessons and . . ."

Tuning her out, I stared off into space. When my gaze focused on a fallen branch in the yard, I wondered idly why Dad hadn't cleared it away, too. I was taking a sip of iced tea when the branch moved. "Snake!" I yelled, spraying tea out my nose as I scrambled to my feet.

Mom shot off the blanket, dragging with her a startled Reenie, who promptly stuck her thumb in her mouth. Jiniwin jumped up, and a deviled egg slid off her plate and landed facedown on her sneaker. Dad snatched up the rake, and Jim Bob grabbed the sickle.

The snake was gigantic, maybe eight feet long, and as big around as a baseball bat. Jim Bob ran over and hacked at it, but with that curved sickle blade, all he could do was make it mad. It reared its head and struck at him.

I was trembling with fear and revulsion, but unable to tear my eyes from the creature writhing on the grass. It was like watching a horror movie, when you can't stand to see the gore but can't stop looking.

"It's only a blacksnake," said Dad. "Don't kill it."

Jim Bob gawked at him. "It's trying to bite me!"

"Put the sickle away, son. We won't need it." Gently, Dad shoved at the snake with the rake and began herding it into an uncut field, as if it were nothing more than a wayward sheep.

"James Robert, are you crazy? Kill it," Mom cried after him in a quavery voice. She was still hanging on to Reenie for dear life.

When Dad came back, he gave Mom an apologetic grin.

"Why'd you let it go?" she demanded.

His hand went to his empty pocket. "Blacksnakes are harmless."

"Harmless, my eye! It was a monster! You saw the way it was fighting Jim Bob!"

"I'd fight, too, if somebody came after me with a sickle. This was his home, you know, until we showed up. From the size of him, he's an old granddaddy, and he deserves to finish his life in peace."

"I don't care if he's old as Methuselah," Mom huffed. "You should have chopped him to bits."

Mom swept furiously, trying to stay one room ahead of Jiniwin and me with our mops. When she finished in the dining room, we were right on her tail. As soon as Jiniwin plopped down our bucket, I sloshed my mop into it and swirled water across the floor.

Mom leaned on her broom and sighed. "Take it easy, girls. You're wearing me down."

"Blame Buddy," said Jiniwin. "I can't keep up with her, either. You'd think she was killing snakes."

"Practicing," I said as I worked the mop. "That granddaddy blacksnake gave me the heebie-jeebies, and I keep thinking we'll find snakes in the house."

"Don't say that," said Mom.

"It could happen. We've got mice. What's to prevent snakes from coming in the same holes?"

"For heaven's sake, Buddy," said Mom, and I could hear the uncertainty in her voice, "if you keep talking like that, you'll make me scared to open a drawer."

I didn't say anything more about snakes, but I felt a grim satisfaction. Maybe there was hope for us yet. I couldn't see my mom and reptiles sharing the same house.

My mop was getting heavier by the minute, and I stood up straight to ease my back. We'd thrown away all the old curtains, and through the tall triple windows, I saw Jim Bob swinging the sickle in the side yard and Dad sauntering out of the barn. Right behind him came Reenie, her brown pong tails bouncing, her slanty eyes squinting in the sunshine. She stopped at a stump in the barn lot. One at a time, she removed the pecan shell critters from the Easter basket and lined them up on the stump. I read her lips as she counted, "One, two, three . . ."

A screeching sound made me jump. It was the back door popping open on rusty hinges.

"Needs a little oil," Dad said as he entered the kitchen. "Irene, come look at my new contraption." Seeing me peering at him from the dining room, he added, "You and Jiniwin, too. You gotta see this."

We gathered around. His contraption was a broomstick with a strip of electrical cord attached. The cord looped through an eyebolt on the end, then ran the entire length of the stick. None of us had a clue as to what we were looking at.

Dad laughed at our blank expressions. "Obviously, you city gals don't recognize this as a snake catcher, so let me demonstrate how it works. Buddy, lay your mop on the floor." I did, and he said, "Now, pretend that's a snake. You take hold of the cord, sneak up on the snake, slip the loop over its head, and *yank*!" When Dad yanked, the mop handle jerked off the floor. He dragged it to the back door and, with one swift motion, loosened the cord and flung the mop onto the porch.

"Very clever, James," said Mom, "as long as the snake holds still."

Dad bowed to her. "My dear, the very next time I find a snake, I'll give you a front-row seat."

"Spare me."

But he didn't. Twice, while we were cleaning upstairs, Dad called us outside for a "snake break." Both times, he caught three-feet-long blacksnakes. Both times, I felt my skin crawl as they writhed and fought mightily with their heads in the noose. Dad carried them a long ways from the house and threw them over a fence into a pasture.

After his second trip, Mom stormed into the house, muttering to herself, "If they're male and female, we'll soon be living in a snake pit."

"It's happening," whispered Jiniwin as we followed her in.

"What's happening?" I asked.

"Your mom changing moods so fast. Your dad humoring those snakes. It's the house. I know it. It's casting a spell."

EIGHT
Too Many Can'ts

THE SUN WAS SETTING as we drove away from Aunt Ruby's, and when Jiniwin turned around to see the witch's head, I looked, too. The weeds and the hog shed were gone. So were the tattered curtains. But the place was still old, tacky, worn out. Although I would have to live there, it would never be home to me.

As Dad hit the bump at the cattle guard, the house's oval window flashed in the sunlight. It winked again. A burning eye.

Jiniwin punched me on the arm, faked a shiver, and made her eyes bug out. The hairs raised at the back of my neck. I frowned at her and shook my head. The last thing I needed was her convincing me the place was haunted.

I didn't relax until we reached Turnback. The town was ablaze with lights welcoming me back to civilization. Headlights. Streetlights. Traffic lights. Store lights. House lights.

When Dad stopped to drop Jiniwin off, the colored squares around her doorway sent a rainbow of light onto the porch. A red Ferrari gleamed in the driveway.

"Ooooh, my car," said Reenie.

Jim Bob whistled softly. "Now that's what I call a set of wheels."

"The guy who drives it's a toad," said Jiniwin, climbing over me to get out. "Thanks, everybody, for letting me tag along."

"Thanks to you for the help," said Mom and Dad.

"Without you, I'd still be swabbing the decks," I said. "Call me after a while, okay? We need to talk about the skating contest."

"Okay. 'Bye." Jiniwin slammed the door and headed slowly up the walk.

"Poor girl," said Mom. "She just can't accept the fact that Paulette isn't ever going to take Frank back."

At our house, we unloaded the car and washed up, and soon we were all flitting around the kitchen—Dad frying hamburgers, Mom making a salad, me filling glasses with ice cubes and tea, Jim Bob and Reenie setting the table. The kitchen was warm and bright, and laughter flowed as we darted back and forth, trying to stay out of each other's way.

"Whatever you do," Dad said after Mom and I had collided twice at the refrigerator, "don't anybody fall down. I'd hate to have to"—he made a scooping motion with the spatula—"scrape you off the floor."

Although I laughed with the others, I felt a nagging sadness because we'd soon be stuck in Aunt Ruby's dreary kitchen.

When we sat down to supper, Mom asked the blessing, then squirted ketchup onto Reenie's plate and said, "They're short-handed at the nursing home. Lana rushed off to Oklahoma because her daughter was hurt in a car wreck, and Jeanie's got the flu. The head nurse wants me to work some days and some nights for the next couple of weeks. Tomorrow I go in at eight."

"It's not right the way she switches you around," said Dad. "With her crazy schedules, you're not getting enough rest."

Mom assured him she could handle it as I piled pickles on my burger. I was taking my first bite when she said, "I think we should start moving tomorrow when I get off work at four."

Tomorrow? Suddenly, that bite was drier than sawdust.

"I thought we'd decided on Wednesday, because that's your day off," Dad said. "I've set it up with Rick to borrow his pickup then, and Jim Bob was going to miss school."

"Wednesday's okay for the heavy stuff," Mom said. "I just want to get a head start."

I managed to swallow the sawdust. "Tomorrow's the skating contest."

"Sorry, hon," Mom said with a weary smile. "You'll have to miss it. You'll be needed here."

So much for my last hurrah. It wouldn't even be a good, healthy grunt. I laid down the hamburger and stared at the grease on the bun. Anger bubbled up inside of me. Every time I turn around, I fumed to myself, I'm being railroaded. Leave this house. Move to the backwoods. Miss the skating contest.

"James," Mom went on, "will you check with Rick about the pickup for tomorrow? While I'm at work, you guys could load the dressers and take down the beds—"

"The beds?" interrupted Jim Bob.

"Leave the mattresses for us to sleep on," Mom told him, then turned to me. "While they're loading, you could empty drawers and closets and pack away anything we can do without. . . ."

As soon as I could get away, I shagged it over to Jiniwin's. By myself. In the dark. At this point, I didn't care about rules.

Jiniwin answered the door. Paulette and her lawyer friend were in the living room, and I barely had time to wave at them before Jiniwin whisked me down the hall to her bedroom. Couldn't blame her. I'd caught a glimpse of myself in the mirrored foyer, and it had almost scared me—hair standing on end, same duds I'd worn all day.

Jiniwin, though, had showered and washed her hair. Once again, she was Miss America. Feeling like a pumpkin among a field of velvet cushions, I dusted off my rump and sat on the bed.

The receiver of Jiniwin's pink phone was lying on the table. She hung it up and said, "I was dialing your number when you rang the doorbell. Think your folks would let you miss church in the morning?"

"Not unless an earthquake destroys the building. Why?"

"So you can go with me to Jefferson City."

"Jefferson City? What about the skating contest?"

Jiniwin shrugged. "I can skate anytime. For once, Paulette and Reginald included me in their plans. I want to go, and I want you to keep me company. It'll be fun—eating ribs at Porky's, touring the capitol, shopping at the mall."

I traced the quilting pattern on the pink bedspread with my finger, which had a half-moon of dirt under the nail. I would have liked seeing the state capitol building, probably just as much as going to the rink, but I couldn't do either one. I tried to swallow the lump in my throat. "I can't go to Jeff City. I can't go to the contest. I have to pack boxes, and *then* I have to unpack them at the witch's head."

Jiniwin didn't say anything at first—just stood twiddling a strand of hair and staring at the pumpkin poster. Finally, she sat beside me on the bed. "Want me to stick around and help?"

She was being a real friend, offering to give up the trip for me. I couldn't let her miss this day with her mom, though, so I shook my head.

"Without you," she said, "I'll probably be bored out of my skull—listening to all that 'honey' and 'sweetheart' stuff between Paulette and Loverboy."

"It'll work out. This may be a once-in-a-lifetime offer, so you'd better grab it."

Mom and Dad, engrossed in a TV show, didn't notice me coming in from outside. I slipped into the foyer and down the hall to my room.

From the doorway, I saw Reenie sitting cross-legged on the floor, playing with the buttons she'd brought from the farm. It hadn't mattered to her that hauling them to town meant we'd just have to haul them back later. She was lining them up underneath her feather tree.

"Nine, ten," she said, then started again with "One, two, three. . . ." There must have been a hundred buttons, and maybe more, but ten was as high as she could count. "Eight, nine, ten."

"After ten comes eleven, twelve, thirteen," I said.

She looked up and smiled as I entered the room. "Yeah, s-sissy. Many buttons."

"You've got many different colors, too. How'd you like to hang buttons on your Christmas tree?"

"Yeah, s-sissy. My tree," she said, and clapped her hands.

I found a darning needle and some thread, and

Reenie and I sat on her bed with Tripod, who was sprawled out and snoozing on the pillow.

I threaded the needle and showed my sister how to run it through the holes in the buttons. She tried hard, slanty eyes squinting, tongue hanging out, but she wasn't coordinated enough to do it. "Can't," she said.

I felt a squeezing in my heart. She'd faced too many "can'ts" in her life. It made me feel small that I, who could do anything I set my mind to, had been feeling sorry for myself. "That's okay. How about if you hand me the buttons, and I'll run them on the string?"

"Yeah-kay, s-sissy."

One at a time, Reenie doled out buttons—flowers, mushrooms, knights, and animals—some smaller than a dime and some as big as a half dollar. Others were in geometric shapes and resembled stained glass. Still others had tiny pictures embedded in black glass.

"You know something, Reenie?" I said as I poked the needle through the face of a man with a mustache and a funny-looking hat. "Mom saves buttons. Cuts them off of old clothes and reuses them. The ones on your shirt used to be on my pajamas."

"Yeah, s-sissy," she said, and she stroked the pearlized buttons on her chest.

"Mom saves *matching* buttons. Aunt Ruby saved a kajillion buttons, and no two are alike."

Reenie just grinned and handed me another button.

We spent about half an hour decorating the tree. When we were finished, it didn't seem quite as scrawny.

"Look, Tripod, my tree," said Reenie, pouncing on the cat. He meowed and stretched and started batting at the buttons.

His antics gave Reenie and me the giggles, and soon Jim Bob stuck his head in the door and asked, "What's all the ruckus?"

"My kitty, Jay-Bob. My tree," said Reenie.

Jim Bob sauntered in and sat on my bed to watch the cat. Soon the three of us were laughing hysterically, and I forgot for a little while that my brother was a pest.

NINE

Country Is . . .

SUNDAY AFTER CHURCH, Dad and Jim Bob and I set to work following Mom's orders. After I emptied drawers, they loaded dressers into the borrowed pickup. While they were loading bedsteads, I emptied closets.

Saying she wanted to "help s-sissy," Reenie trailed after me like a shadow, and her help consisted of taking out and showing me things I'd just packed in a box.

In a basket at the back of our closet, I found Jim Bob's old Mattel See 'n' Say talking toy. Recalling how Reenie had driven me up the wall with it a couple of years before, I tried to hide it. I wasn't fast enough.

"My toy!" she exclaimed, latching on to it and pulling the string.

The pointer spun around and stopped at the picture of a pig. A mechanical voice said, "Here is a pig . . ." and paused. We heard a grinding noise, and the voice said, "Quack-quack, quack-quack."

Tripod howled, and Reenie turned her puzzled eyes on me.

"That thing's ancient. Worn out. It doesn't know a pig from a duck."

She pulled the string again.

"Here is a horse. . . ." Pause, grind. "Arf, arf."

Tripod yowled mournfully as we went through the whole mixed-up barnyard scene. A chicken meowing, a bird mooing, a dog crowing, a cat oinking. On and on it went.

Just when I thought I'd blow my stack, Mom stuck her head in the door and said, "I'm home."

"My farm," said Reenie, and she ran to her with the See 'n' Say.

"Uh-oh." Mom grinned at me as she hugged my sister. "Are your ears tired?"

"I'll say. If I hear a duck moo one more time, I'll quack up."

Mom chuckled. "Come help me pack my good dishes. I'm glad we still have those old newspapers."

In the kitchen, Reenie sat at the table and pulled the string on the See 'n' Say. When a horse oinked, Mom said, "That poor old thing," and climbed up onto the countertop. She was handing dishes down to me when the phone rang.

I answered and talked to Aunt Sage, who'd been watching Dad and Jim Bob at the pickup. When she hinted that she'd like to get in on the action, I invited her to go along for the unloading.

"Why, Buddy, that's real sweet of you. I've been cooped up in this house for a month of Sundays."

"We'll pick you up in a few minutes. And, Aunt Sage?"

"Yes, Buddy."

"Don't forget to hang up the phone."

"Of course, I won't forget. I'm not senile."

Dad and Jim Bob rode in the pickup out to Aunt Ruby's, while the rest of us followed in the station wagon. Naturally, I took Miss Molly along.

Aunt Sage, wearing a blue polyester pantsuit and a crocheted vest, sat in the front seat, clutching her crocheted pocketbook and gawking at the sights. When we passed the Benge mailbox, she said, "It was a sad day when Wilma Benge died so young, leaving her boy behind."

"I didn't know she died," said Mom.

"Cancer."

"Was the boy's name Dallas?" I asked.

"Why, yes, it was. Do you know him? I've often wondered how he's fared."

Dallas was so nice to Reenie, I couldn't bring myself to report that he dug through trash and sold his pickings at the flea market. "His name's always on the honor roll," I said. "I guess he's doing okay."

Aunt Sage gave a "harumph" and yanked at the ties

of her vest. "With no help from his dad, I'll wager. Wilma never got anything but grief. I never could figure out how she got mixed up with a drunk like Lewis Benge. When she was a little girl, she'd come to the farm with her daddy to buy milk. She'd pet the dogs and watch the cows and dream her special dreams. She wanted to own a cattle ranch in Texas. The closest she ever got was naming that boy 'Dallas.' "

Mom was slowing down to cross Aunt Ruby's cattle guard. "You know," she said softly, "with the weeds cut and the hog shed gone, this place looks almost presentable."

"So this is the farm," breathed Aunt Sage, and I knew she was remembering Herbert and their dairy farm.

"My farm," said Reenie. She pulled the string on the See 'n' Say, and we bounced up the road to the sound of a whinnying rooster.

When Mom stopped the car, Reenie bailed out running.

"Where you going, Flash?" asked Jim Bob as he got out of the pickup.

"My payno," she called over her shoulder. She made a bee-line for the backyard, and there she stayed, singing and banging on the piano while Mom gave Aunt Sage a tour of the house and I trailed along behind with Miss Molly.

When we returned to the kitchen, Aunt Sage said, "You've got plenty of cabinets."

"But they're so dark, they make the kitchen gloomy," Mom replied. "I want to paint them a pale green and stencil vines along the edges. Give them the country look."

I almost snorted. The country look was everywhere. No neighbors for a quarter of a mile. A dilapidated smokehouse in the backyard. A claw-foot bathtub with rust streaks and no shower.

Mom walked over and touched Aunt Ruby's ancient cookstove. "I'll have to get used to cooking with gas. My electric range stays with the house in town."

That was news to me. I glanced away from the stove and out the window at my sister. "It's got burners."

"Dad and I've already thought of that. We'll just have to keep the knobs in a drawer. Put them on only when we want to cook."

I supposed that would work. Someone who couldn't run a needle through a button probably couldn't insert a knob on the stove.

"At least this one's got a bigger oven," Mom said. She opened the oven door, then jumped back, shrieking, "Snake!"

As I shied away backward, a thought flashed through my mind: Country is a snake in the oven.

Aunt Sage tottered over for a peek. "Why, Irene, that's just a little old blacksnake."

"I don't care if it's an earthworm. I want it out of my house. Buddy, go get Dad."

I ran and fetched him, and he retrieved the snake

catcher from its nail on the back porch and promptly disposed of the snake.

When he came back inside, Mom was leaning on the cabinet and staring at the stove. "James, I'll put up with a lot, but I just can't abide having snakes in the house."

"It's the mice, hon. As soon as we get rid of the mice, the snakes'll leave of their own accord. Then I'll patch the holes where they're getting in."

"Maybe you should have left the hog shed where it was," said Aunt Sage.

"Why?" asked Dad.

"Hogs kill snakes. My guess is, Ruby wanted the hogs up close to the house 'cause she had so many blacksnakes."

Mom moaned and clapped her hands over her ears. "Don't say that. If I come across another one, I'll have a heart attack for sure."

Reenie and I rode home with Dad in Rick's pickup. At the entrance gates of Turnback Heights, she punched Dad on the shoulder and said, "Around the horn, Dod."

He grinned at her. "You don't ask for much. I guess I can handle one little ride around the horn."

Reenie giggled and clapped her hands as he started driving the complete circle around the subdivision. "Play ball," she said, pointing at the whole Archer family enjoying a game of volleyball. "Pretty car," she said, referring to Mr. Walburn washing his Oldsmobile.

I'd never given much thought before to why Reenie liked riding around the horn. I'd just assumed it was another one of her quirks. Now, as I watched her watching the neighbors, I realized she appreciated them as much as I did.

At home, while Dad and Jim Bob were returning the pickup, Mom and I went to work fixing a salad and grilled cheese sandwiches. When Reenie switched on the TV, Mom sent me in to find a good show for her to watch. Scary ones gave her bad dreams.

After supper, Reenie followed me to our room. "Mess," she said.

It *was* a mess, and it didn't feel like our room anymore. The furniture was gone, the closet almost empty. The mattresses on the floor held tangled heaps of bedclothes. In the corner lay a scattering of dollars, dumped there carelessly when Dad and Jim Bob moved the dresser.

While I straightened our sheets and blankets, Reenie picked up her rocks. Counting over and over from one to ten, she arranged them neatly on the floor. "My dollars," she sang. "Many dollars."

The rocks were in line now, and so was her world. I wished I could say the same about mine.

"Anybody home?" asked Jiniwin from the doorway, her arms full of packages.

"Hi. Come on in." Seeing a haziness in her eyes, I added, "Are you okay? You look kind of feverish."

"No fever. I'm just bored out of my gourd. That Reginald is a drag." Jiniwin dumped her packages on my mattress and sat next to them. "I came to show you the loot I got in Jeff City." From the bags, she pulled out a pink sweater, pink tennis shoes, pink necklace, a pink purse for Reenie, and matching pink T-shirts that said SHOP TILL YOU DROP for her and me.

"My purse! Pretty purse!" exclaimed Reenie as she grabbed it and started flinging out wads of paper stuffing.

"She likes it," chuckled Jiniwin.

But I wasn't crazy about my T-shirt. I fingered its soft fabric. Not only was the shirt too small, but I never wore pink, because of my red hair. Didn't Jiniwin remember how I'd fought tooth-and-nail in sixth-grade chorus when the other girls wanted pink dresses?

"Look, Jivven. Farm," said Reenie. She pulled the string of the See 'n' Say, and a chicken mooed.

Jiniwin burst into hysterical laughter. Mooing and squawking, she jumped off the mattress and started flapping her arms and hopping around the room.

Talk about overreaction. I was dumbfounded.

Finally, Jiniwin calmed down, collapsed onto my mattress, and swatted the matching T-shirts. "Well, whadda you think?"

I couldn't tell a lie, so I thought fast. "I—they—they're really pretty. The color's just perfect for you."

TEN

New Kids on the Bus

THE WEEK STARTED OUT WRONG and went downhill from there.

On Monday, walking to school, Reenie invited everyone we met to "Come to my house. Come to the farm." Time and time again, I had to explain about our moving, plus give the lowdown on the egg in the basket. It was the same story on the way home. Not only that, but Jiniwin had insisted that we wear our matching T-shirts. All day long, I was self-conscious, knowing I looked like a bag of link sausages.

Tuesday, my English homework got trampled in the hallway, lunch was mystery meat and creamed peas, and I broke a bra strap in P.E. Then, when I got home from school, I saw the writing wall propped behind the couch.

I slammed the door and stood motionless in the foyer, wanting to burst into tears. All along, I'd harbored a tiny hope that Mom wouldn't be able to leave our home and all its memories behind. I felt cheated, almost, that the writing wall had been ripped out and moved like a piece of furniture. My parents could dismantle the whole house, move every board and shingle, but they could never move my heart.

"In here, girls," Mom called from the hallway.

Reenie was tugging impatiently on my arm, but still I didn't move. The smell of peach surprise, mingled with that of household cleaner and wood glue, was turning my stomach inside out.

Finally, I gave in to Reenie's tugging, and we rounded the corner into the hallway.

Mom was wiping something off the floor, and Dad was smearing glue on the wall. Next to him stood a new sheet of paneling.

"Wall?" said Reenie.

"That's right, hon," Dad replied. "I know how much that writing wall means to your mother. That's why we're taking it to the farm."

"You girls want some peach surprise?" Mom asked as she dropped her sponge into a bucket and got up.

"Not hungry," I grunted, brushing past her and aiming for my room.

Dad blocked my way. "That's no way to greet your mother. Go back and try again."

Resisting the urge to heave a deep sigh, I apologized. "Sorry, Mom. I'll pass on the surprise."

I barely made it to my mattress before the tears erupted. If a person really could drown in her own sorrow, I would have been a goner. As it was, I ended up with a stuffy nose and burning eyes and hiccups.

Eventually, I sat up, propped my chin on the windowsill, and stared at the tree house in the backyard. I didn't want strange kids playing in it and sending secret messages. After a while, I went out and climbed the tree and took the pulley down.

I woke up feeling miserable Wednesday morning. It was almost more than I could do to wash my face, pull on a pair of jeans and one of Dad's chambray shirts, and comb my hair. I roamed from room to room, telling the house good-bye. I saw Reenie admiring herself in the bathroom, and I thought, That's the last time she'll ever look in that mirror. I saw the windowpanes around the front door, and I wondered if the new owners would stencil them with snowflakes.

At breakfast, while Dad and Jim Bob planned their strategy for moving the refrigerator and the deep freeze, I choked down a few bites of sausage. If this keeps up, I thought gloomily, maybe I'll drop a few pounds.

Wiping egg off Reenie's face, Mom said, "Buddy will pick you up as usual when school's out, and you girls'll ride the bus to the farm."

"My bus? My farm?"

"That's right." Turning to me, Mom said, "Your bus is number thirteen."

"That figures."

"You're such an old sobersides," she said. "Don't

worry so much. You'll adjust to these changes. We all will. You'll see."

I didn't answer at the time, but later, brushing my teeth, I thought of what she'd said, and I muttered, "When pigs fly."

At school, I managed to keep a seat warm, but I couldn't keep my mind on my lessons. If teachers spoke to me, they had to repeat what they'd said. All I could think of was that when this day was over, I'd have no home to go home to.

Mrs. Royal tried to help, seventh hour. When I missed nine out of twenty on a trial test, she called me to her desk.

I stood before her, staring at the floor, feeling twenty pairs of eyes boring into my back. I hoped Dad's shirt was hiding all the bulges.

"Look at me," Mrs. Royal said softly, so no one else could hear.

Starting at her feet, I worked my way up. Thick ankles, thick legs, thick body in a green-and-white striped dress, mousy brown hair to her shoulders. I looked briefly at her eyes, magnified by the thick lenses of her glasses, then focused on the mole above the nosepiece.

She tapped my test paper. "Buddy, this isn't like you. Didn't you study your notes?"

"Yes, ma'am. Last night."

"Is there a problem here at school?"

"No, ma'am."

"Is something wrong at home?"

"No. Yes. We're moving. I don't want to go."

"Out of the school district?"

"No. Just out of town."

"Well, that's one teensy bright spot anyway. I think you could use a visit to the lab. Go in and talk to the animals. Let me know if they talk back."

She was trying to make me smile. I couldn't. I mumbled, "Thanks," and fled from the room, just as the ten-minute bell rang.

As usual, the lab was brightly lit. What was it like for these creatures, always being in the spotlight? Just that few minutes at the front of the room with Mrs. Royal had been enough for me. To the animals in general, I announced, "Nobody asked you about it, right, guys? They just snagged you in a net and locked you in a cage."

Ignoring the iguana, the snake, and the alligator, I headed straight for Precious. The little guinea pig was gnawing on his feeding tray. I leaned my elbows on his glass cage and stared down through the wire top. "Well, Precious, I'm supposed to talk to you. I'm supposed to let my gentle feelings come out. How's this for gentle? How about if we send Jaws back to Florida? Flush Goomer down the toilet? Turn Jake loose in the principal's office?"

Precious stopped gnawing and stared at me with his black, beady eyes.

I couldn't help but laugh. "Got your attention, hey, boy?" After pushing aside the wire, I reached into the cage and stroked his tan, furry body. When he sniffed at my fingers, I picked him up and nuzzled him against my neck. His whiskers tickled.

"Why do they call you a guinea pig? A guinea is a bird. A pig is a pig. You're more like a mouse than anything else."

Precious crawled onto my shoulder, digging in with his little feet. I giggled when he nibbled my ear.

"Let me tell you a secret. I'm madder than hops right now, because I have to leave my home. You know what that's like. You had to leave your home and be locked up in a dumb old cage."

Precious started nibbling my other ear.

"I could also tell you how sad I was when Reenie and I walked to school with my best friend for the last time. I could tell you how I'm going to hate having to ride on a school bus."

The bell rang. School was over. I petted the guinea pig once more, put him in his cage, and replaced the wire cover. " 'Bye, Precious."

To my amazement, he placed a paw on the glass, almost as if he were waving.

"Feeling better?" Mrs. Royal asked from the doorway.

I turned and smiled at her. Maybe it was the light, but her hair didn't look quite so mousy, and she actually seemed less dumpy in stripes.

"I'll go with you to pick up Reenie," said Jiniwin.

"Okay," I replied, backing out of my locker with Miss Molly and an armload of books.

As we left the building, Jiniwin said, "I don't even have to ask. I can tell by the look on your face that it helped to talk to Mrs. Royal's menagerie."

"Not the whole menagerie, just Precious."

"He's a good listener. When I tell him about Paulette and Loverboy Lawyer, he never interrupts."

"He's got such beady, intelligent eyes."

"I know, but Paulette's gonna stick with him anyway."

We broke up laughing, and were still laughing when we reached Reenie.

She jumped up, swinging her sequin purse, and told Mrs. Houston, "My s-sissy happy."

"I see that. What's so funny, girls?"

"A lawyer with guinea-pig eyes," I said, and Jiniwin and I hooted with laughter again.

However, when we found bus number thirteen, engine belching and exhaust stinking, I sobered up fast. About a dozen kids were yelling out the windows, from which paper airplanes swooped out and up, then crashed. A spitball landed at my feet with a splat.

"I'd rather be in a cage with Jaws than ride that stupid bus," I muttered.

Jiniwin gave a sympathetic nod. "Call me later? So I'll know if you survived."

"If they installed the phone."

The driver revved up the engine and called out the door, "You girls Richters?"

I nodded, and he said, "You waiting for a limousine, or what?"

I rolled my eyes at Jiniwin, then took Reenie's hand and climbed up the steps.

I saw no empty seats. Only bodies and a sea of faces. Everybody was gawking at us, the new kids.

Behind me, the driver said, "Can't move until you girls are seated. Preferably before we all turn to stone like the petrified forest."

I pulled Reenie down the aisle. All around us, mouths were flapping:

"Little Red Riding Hood, what's in the basket?"

"Where's your ticket? Gotta have a ticket to ride this crate."

"Can you believe it? Sucking her thumb?"

"She's a retard."

I glowered at the girl who said that—a high school student I knew only as Loretta. With an evil grin, she said, "Duh-uhhh," and slowly, deliberately, stuck her thumb in her mouth.

Face hot, eyes blind with rage, I towed Reenie on down the aisle.

Someone grabbed my arm and said, "Here. Sit here." It was Dallas Benge.

Gratefully, I guided Reenie into the seat and plunged in beside her.

"Hi, boy," she said.

"Hi to you, too," said Dallas.

A grimy kid with two teeth missing reached over the seat and tweaked Reenie's pong tails, and she turned around and ordered, "Hands off."

"Oooh, I'm scared," the boy said, and tweaked her hair again.

Dallas fixed him with a cold stare. "You heard the little lady. Hands off."

"All right, Dallath," he lisped. "Don't get exthited."

Dallas glared at him for a moment longer, then turned to me. "How come you're on the bus?"

"We're moving," I said, vaguely aware of a scent I couldn't identify. As the bus pulled away, I glanced around at all the confusion. "Is it always this bad?"

"Yeah, at least until we drop off a few kids. Everybody's all wound up after school. But they're pretty tame in the mornings."

"Well, thanks for sharing your seat."

"No problem. Nobody ever sits with Dallas Benge. They're afraid of getting cooties."

My eyes darted toward his straight brown hair.

He noticed, and tousled his hair with both hands. "Bushy-headed, maybe, but no cooties. At least not today."

"I'm sorry. I didn't mean to—"

"It's okay. I'm the one who mentioned cooties." Dallas's ears were beet red as he turned his attention to Reenie. "Hmmmm, a sequin purse. Now where have I seen that before?"

She beamed at him and opened the purse to reveal all the rocks inside. "My dollars. Many dollars."

Dallas gave a low whistle and proceeded to count all her "money."

I took the opportunity to really study him, close up. Long and lean. Dark, shadowy brown eyes. Wrinkled Cardinals T-shirt with the logo peeling off. Windbreaker tied around his waist. Faded jeans. Sneakers with no socks.

With surprise, I noticed that his ankles were clean. For some reason, I'd expected them to be dirt-encrusted. Then I remembered why. Jiniwin had said he smelled like dirt and mustard. My eyes dropped down to his books on the floor and the neatly folded lunch sack. Mustard sandwiches, she'd said. I recognized the scent then—a combination of mustard and earth. Not dirt, but the fresh, clean scent of damp earth after a rain.

Earth, as in grave. I pictured Dallas standing at his mother's grave, and suddenly, I felt sorry for him. I wondered if he had any friends at school, any relatives besides his drunken dad. Of course, I couldn't ask, but still, I wanted to say something. "Dallas?"

"Yeah?"

"We're your new neighbors. My family's moving to my great-aunt Ruby's place. Ruby Richter. I think your mom cooked for her."

At the mention of his mother, Dallas's eyes flickered with sadness, and I wished for a bar of soap to wash out my mouth.

"Mom liked your Aunt Ruby," he said. "She liked the farm."

Reenie slapped him on the leg. "Come to my house. Come to the farm."

"It's not really a farm anymore," I said. "No crops. No animals. All we've got is a three-legged cat named Tripod."

"I've got a pet raccoon. Major D. That's short for Major Disaster."

I laughed. "How'd you come up with a name like that?"

"He caused a major disaster when I brought him home. You see, he was just a little thing when I snagged him with a towel down at the creek. I put him in my dad's pickup and went to build a cage. He tore up the truck. Clawed up the dashboard. Ripped off a door panel. Pulled the stuffing out of the seat."

"What'd your dad say?"

"Censored. He was drunk, and he worked me over with his belt." At my horrified expression, Dallas added, "I didn't mind so much, 'cause I got to keep Major D. I hid him until the old man sobered up, and he never said any more about it. I figure he was so drunk, he thought he'd damaged the truck himself."

"Reenie would love Major D. Could I bring her over to see him sometime?"

"No! You stay away from our property!"

I jerked my head back and gaped at him. His eyes were narrowed, his cheeks splotched with red.

"I don't mean to be hateful, but get this straight, Buddy. You've got to *stay away*."

Don't worry, I thought as I looked away from those

angry eyes. I wouldn't come if my life depended on it. Folding my arms, I stared toward the front of the bus. What was this guy's problem? One minute he was rescuing us from the mob; the next, he was incredibly rude.

"Here, boy. Dollar," said Reenie, and from the corner of my eye, I saw her give Dallas a rock.

He accepted it and stored it away in his lunch sack. "Once in a while, I find shiny rocks at the creek or the mining pit," he said. "I'll start saving them for you."

"Yeah, boy. My dollars."

They kept a conversation going until we reached Dallas's mailbox. " 'Bye, Reenie," he said when the bus stopped. He climbed over us, then turned and looked down at me. "Save me a seat tomorrow?"

"What?"

"The route is reversed in the mornings. You'll get on before me." When I didn't reply, he asked again, "Save me a seat?"

"There'll be plenty of seats in the morning. You won't have to sit with me."

"I want to."

"Benge," growled the driver, "I'm petrifying up here."

Dallas looked at me, waiting for an answer. I stared him down. He shook his head, got off the bus, and stopped to check the rusty mailbox.

As the bus started moving, the boy who'd tweaked Reenie's pong tails yelled out the window, "Hey, junk man, what'd you get? A bunch of junk mail?"

ELEVEN
No-Man's-Land

THE BUS DRIVER LET US OFF at the cattle guard, told us what time he'd be by in the morning, and pulled away in a fog of dust and diesel exhaust.

Reenie and I walked slowly up the road toward the witch's head. Its tall, old-fashioned windows now looked like hooded eyes, because someone had hung our drapes from town, and they were much too short to cover all the glass. Boxes lay haphazardly on the porch. That bright splash of color on the weathered siding was our nameplate. I couldn't read the writing, but I knew very well what it said: "A house is just a house, but a home is filled with love."

"It'll never be home," I muttered.

"My home. My farm."

I smiled wistfully at my happy-go-lucky sister. "Put the old charmer to work, Reenie. I need some of your good nature to rub off on me."

"Yeah, s-sissy." At the walkway, Reenie stooped down to pick up some rocks.

With a sigh, I waited for her to drop them into her purse; then we went on to the house.

The living room seemed cavernous, since half of it was empty. At one end, our couch, chairs, tables, and TV had been arranged neatly, and even the afghan was doing its job of hiding the lumps in the couch. From upstairs came thumping and banging. The air smelled stale and musty—not a bit like home.

Mom came in, all smiles as she dried her hands on a towel. "Hi, girls. What do you think of the room?" Her face was shiny with sweat, and strands of wiry red hair were glued to her forehead.

She wanted me to say it was cozy or something. All I could manage was, "You've done a lot."

"Had to. Tomorrow I go back to work." Mom kissed Reenie and me, then herded us to the kitchen. "It's not the Ritz—yet," she said.

The Ritz? Who cared about living in a fancy hotel? All I wanted was our own house back. My eyes swept the kitchen. I saw windows without curtains, a stove with the burner knobs missing, dishes and cans on the counter, a package of Oreos on our Formica-topped table, a new black wall telephone.

How I wanted to call Jiniwin. I'd missed walking home with her and hashing over who did what at school. I needed to tell her about Dallas, have her help me figure out how he could be so nice one minute and so rude the next. But I knew I couldn't call just yet—not until I'd helped Mom with the house.

As Reenie and I sat down at the table, Mom turned on the tap and let the water run. "How was school today?"

"School was so-so," I said, handing two cookies to Reenie and taking one for myself. "The bus was the pits. Everybody staring and yelling, and one girl called Reenie an R-E-T-A-R-D." I could never bring myself to say "retard." It was an ugly word.

"I'll call the bus driver and put a stop to that nonsense," Mom said as she plunked down two glasses of water for Reenie and me.

"Not yet. Probably after the new wears off, everybody'll find another goat to pick on."

Mom climbed on a stool and started shoving bowls into the cupboard. "I don't know, Buddy. Some people are like chickens in a barnyard. They gang up against one little hen, and they pick and poke and peck her to death."

"Reenie's not a chicken, and I'm not either, and if Loretta what's-her-face smarts off one more time, she'll find out."

"Kitty?" said Reenie, who'd reserved a bite of cookie for Tripod.

"He's here somewhere," Mom replied. "He's probably hiding, tired of getting stepped on. . . . Hey, what's this?" She lifted the lid of a casserole dish, and the smell of Texas hash wafted across the kitchen. "Aunt Sage must have sent this out with Jim Bob."

I ate another Oreo and washed it down. "This water tastes funny," I said, holding the glass up to the light.

"No chemicals. Icy cold and straight out of the ground. Oh, Buddy, we're going to love this place. We'll plant a garden in the spring. Maybe buy a cow and some chickens. You know—get back to nature, with our own vegetables, milk, and eggs. It'll be so good for all of us."

When pigs fly, I thought, and imagined myself tanning hides and weaving cloth.

"The house was cold this morning, and your dad wanted to fire up the wood stove," Mom said. "I talked him out of that. No sense rushing the season. You can't shut off a wood stove, and we'd have melted down like wax."

The noise upstairs grew louder, and the whole house seemed to shake. I frowned at the ceiling. "Is the roof caving in, or what?"

"The guys are reassembling the beds. I refuse to sleep on just a mattress here. We'd probably have mice crawling into bed with us."

Or snakes. The words were unspoken, but the message was there on our faces.

Unable to find Tripod, Reenie headed for the back door, saying, "My payno. My music."

I eyed the phone again, and was startled when it rang.

"Would you get—" Mom began, but I was already reaching for the receiver. "Hello?"

"Buddy?" said Aunt Sage. "Just checking to see if Jim Bob got home without spilling that casserole. It was riding on the seat."

"It's fine, and it smells delicious. You were sweet to think of us."

"How could I not think of you? You're like family."

"Thanks. You are, too."

After hanging up the phone, I asked Mom what she wanted me to do, and she sent me upstairs to organize Reenie's and my room. In our doorway, I stopped and looked inside. My posters would hide that Africa-shaped stain on the wallpaper. Maybe curtains would make the brown roses less noticeable.

Seeing a movement at the corner of my eye, I immediately thought "snake." It was Tripod in the middle of my bed, worrying a mouse with his paws. When he saw me, he snatched it up in his mouth protectively.

"Tripod!" I cried. "Get out!"

He leaped off the bed and streaked past me into the hall with the mouse. I walked over and examined the mattress. No blood. No guts. Still, the Oreos in my stomach did a somersault.

It was stuffy up here, and everything smelled old. Will we ever get rid of that smell? I wondered as I knelt on the window seat and opened one of the windows. The sash slid down again, and I pushed it back up. Down. Up. With a sigh, I rummaged around in a box to find something to use as a prop.

With a dictionary holding the window up, I leaned my forearms on the sill and looked out. Reenie's piano tree blocked part of my view, but her voice came floating up to me. "My payno. My music. My farm." I listened for a minute as I peered down through the leaves. I could see a tractor half-hidden by weeds. A broken rail fence. That heap of trash, still waiting to be burned. Deep woods behind the barn.

Sighing again, I turned away from the window and got to work. I put clean sheets on the beds, unpacked clothing from boxes, arranged rocks around Reenie's feather tree on the dresser. I even summoned up my courage to open the window seat. No mice. No snakes. We'd thrown away the junk, and the hole yawned long and narrow, coffinlike.

Suddenly, I ached to talk to Jiniwin, and I hurried downstairs, hoping Mom was finished in the kitchen. The counter was tidy, Mom was gone, and I smelled the Texas hash warming in the oven. I snatched up the phone. Instead of a dial tone, I heard a commercial about scrubbing bubbles, which could mean only one thing—Aunt Sage had forgotten to hang up again.

The screen door squeaked open, and Mom stuck her head inside. Her face was white, her blue eyes round as marbles. "Reenie's gone."

I froze.

"We've got to find her. It'll be dark soon."

"I—we—where do we start?"

"I'll check the property. You take the road. She can't have gone far," Mom said, but both she and I knew Reenie could disappear into thin air. In a flash.

I raced through the house and out the front door. As I ran along the graveled walkway, I glanced right and left, praying I'd catch a glimpse of Reenie's blue shirt. Nothing.

I ran to the pond and stopped to scan its banks, though I was pretty sure Reenie couldn't climb the fence. Still nothing.

Down the road and across the cattle guard. Would Reenie go straight, or would she turn right and explore a place she hadn't been before? I trotted straight ahead and topped a rise, and when I didn't see my sister, I turned around and trotted the other way.

Around the bend on the gravel road was all new territory to me, a no-man's-land. The branches of giant trees met overhead, creating a tunnel that seemed cold and dark and foreboding. Would Reenie have come this way? And what guarantee did I have that she'd even stay on the road? There were no fences along here, so she could have wandered off and gotten lost in the woods, or drowned in one of those clay pits. What if she'd scrounged up some matches and was this minute setting the woods on fire?

I ran until I couldn't run anymore, until I was dizzy from cranking my head from side to side, until the bottoms of my feet were sore from the gravel digging into my shoes. I didn't find Reenie.

My heart was pounding crazily in my chest. Darkness was falling, and the air was turning cold. Choking back a sob, I started back to the house.

Soon I heard Jim Bob calling my name.

"Here!" I yelled.

He met me on the road. "The Flash is safe and sound. She was in the barn with Tripod. Hey, are you all right? You look sick."

"I'm okay."

He put his arm around me and kept it there until we reached the cattle guard. I was too tired and weak to be surprised.

When we got back to the house, Dad and Reenie were playing with the See 'n' Say in the kitchen.

Thank you, Lord, I prayed silently, and sank into a chair. Mom had set the table and was pulling the Texas hash from the oven with her checkered mitts. The globe light fixture was bathing the table in a warm glow, shining on our Melmac dishes. If I squinted my eyes, I could almost pretend we were back home, back to normal. But that was wishful thinking. Nothing would ever be normal again, not with a whole wilderness out there just waiting to swallow Reenie up.

When supper was over, I tried again to call Jiniwin. Aunt Sage's phone was still off the hook.

Later, I had trouble sleeping in a strange room. The old house creaked and groaned. An owl hooted, and frogs croaked down at the pond. Some unnamed beasts were yapping and yowling on the run, their cries fading in and out like sirens. A rustling sound in the room reminded me that Jiniwin thought the house was haunted. Was that a snake in the window seat, or the passing of a ghost?

The rustling turned into the scritching of little claws. I thought of the mouse on the bed. Tripod. A raccoon named Major Disaster.

Why had Dallas been so adamant about me staying away from his house? A simple, "I'm not allowed to have company," would have gotten his message across.

Maybe he was ashamed. Maybe the place was filthy, with flea market junk everywhere. Maybe his dad was a raving maniac who took potshots at visitors.

Would I save Dallas a seat in the morning? I didn't know. I fell asleep, remembering how he'd promised to pick up shiny rocks for Reenie.

TWELVE
Dallas

THURSDAY MORNING, Mom woke me early. "Dad's driving me to work," she said, "but first we're going by the house to double-check the closets and pick up the last load of boxes. You've got to catch the bus, so don't let Reenie dawdle."

But that was easier said than done.

Reenie wanted her "wellow" shirt, and I couldn't find it anywhere. "Come on," I begged. "Wear this purple one."

"Wellow."

"It's not here. It's probably still in town. You can wear it tomorrow."

"Wellow."

I folded the purple shirt and put it back in the drawer. "I guess you'll just have to stay home then. You won't get to ride the bus."

"My bus."

"Not today. Can't ride in your jammies."

She put on the purple shirt, but then I had to help her find a purse to match it before she'd let me fix her pong tails.

That left me with twenty-one minutes to get myself ready and rummage up some breakfast, a job Dad normally did. I threw on a pair of jeans and a striped blouse, then passed the brush through my hair as I flew down the stairs. Through the dining room window, I saw Jim Bob disappearing into the barn, probably for another look at Aunt Ruby's old pickup.

I made cinnamon toast and poured two glasses of milk, and while Reenie and I were eating, Jim Bob moseyed in to ask, "How long before our chariot gets here?"

"Five minutes. Hurry, Reenie. Eat up. Then brush your teeth and put your jacket on. It's time to go."

"Yeah-kay, s-sissy," she said, bending down to pet Tripod and give him a piece of crust.

I frisked her while she brushed her teeth. Her pockets were empty, but she'd stashed a burner knob in her purse. "Reenie Richter," I said, holding up the knob, "what's the meaning of this?"

"My fire."

"It's Mom's fire, and we have to leave it here."

Somehow, we made it to the cattle guard just as the

bus was pulling up. Reenie jumped on eagerly and sat down near the front. I climbed over her with Miss Molly and sat by the window, and I noticed Loretta watching Jim Bob, who was going all the way to the back.

"Are you Jim Bob's *sisters*?" Loretta asked as the driver raked the gears and set the bus in motion.

I fixed her with a glare. "We all crawled out of the same swamp."

She blushed a brilliant purple, and I smiled to myself. So Loretta had eyes for Jim Bob. He'd heard about the "retard" business, and he wouldn't give her the time of day.

At Dallas's stop, I saw him standing by the mailbox in jeans and a plaid flannel shirt that needed ironing. Saw his straight brown hair riffling in the breeze. Clean and feathery.

He climbed onto the bus and just stood in the aisle looking at me.

Still feeling good about Loretta, I smiled. He smiled back.

"Hi, boy," said Reenie, scooting over and patting the seat.

When Dallas and I got off the bus at the junior-senior high, I noticed a girl sitting on a bench with a couple of high school boys. She was so painted up with mascara and eye shadow and plum-colored rouge that I didn't recognize her as Jiniwin until she stood and yelled for me to wait up.

I stopped walking, but Dallas said, "See you after school on the Orient Express," and kept going.

"Okay." I noticed that his ears were bright red. Boy, did he ever have a crush on Jiniwin.

She marched up to me, saying, "Buddy Rae Richter, why are you hanging out with Dallas Benge right here in front of the whole school?"

I backed away from her bad breath. "Hanging out? That's crazy. We got off the same bus. Actually, I tried to call you last night so you could help me figure him out, but I couldn't get through."

"Same here. I wore a blister on my finger trying to call you."

"Aunt Sage struck again. Next time, all you have to do is run over and hang up her phone."

"No way. It's impossible to get away from that old lady."

"Were you calling just to talk?"

"Yeah, at first. You know how the house spooks me. Then when Paulette called and said she was staying in Kansas City, I wanted to come out and spend the night. I would have ridden my bike out, except it was already almost dark and I wasn't sure I knew the way. I checked out the gl—"

She stopped herself before saying "globe." Did she think I'd make fun of her for trying to "find" her mother? All at once, I felt guilty for moving, for leaving her in the lurch. "You must have made out all right. You survived."

Jiniwin snorted. "Locked all the windows and

doors. Made a barricade out of my dresser. Lay awake half the night and prayed the bogeyman wouldn't get me."

"So that's why all the makeup?"

"Does it look bad? I woke up with another headache. Felt like death warmed over this morning."

"Well, no, not bad. It's just not you, is all."

"So tell me, how was your first night in the boonies?"

"It could have been worse. We lost Reenie for a while, but she was just in the barn. I lay awake worrying about mice and snakes and ghosts. Pretty stupid, considering what you went through."

"How was the bus ride?"

"Cruddy. Kids pestering Reenie. Dallas made one boy leave her alone."

"Dallas again? That guy's falling for you."

"Don't be ridiculous. He likes Reenie. They're pals." I told her how his mood had changed when he thought I might drop in at his house.

"Just be careful," she said.

"Careful of what?"

"Getting too close to him. You don't want to start smelling like dirt and mustard."

Jiniwin and I had started a fad when we decorated Miss Molly and Groucho. Only three students in our family living class still had plain white eggs. Lonnie Joe Ross had painted his to look like himself—curly black hair, green eyes, a gap between the teeth. I was more than a little curious that afternoon when he walked in with nothing in his hands.

"As you know," Mrs. Blatterman said, "next Thursday is D-Day, when the condition of your babies will make or break your grades."

"That's the thirteenth," piped Jiniwin. "Can't we wait until the fourteenth, in case some of us are superstitious?"

"No, we can't. You know very well that school is out on the fourteenth for parent-teacher conferences. I timed D-Day for the thirteenth so I can report to your parents what kind of parents *you* turned out to be."

The whole class responded in a caterwauling groan.

"You're not fooling me," said the teacher. "I know, by the ways you've personalized your babies, that you're really falling into the groove. Look around. We've got faces from A to Z. Theresa has an Abraham Lincoln, and Roy has a Ziggy. There are rainbows and polka-dots and—" Abruptly, she stopped talking and marched over to Lonnie Joe's desk.

Every eye in the class riveted on Lonnie Joe as she asked, "Where's your child, young man?"

"I don't have it."

"You mean you left it at home?"

"No. I left it in my mom's car, and somebody stole it. A prank, I guess. Why else would anybody steal an egg?"

"You left a poor, defenseless baby all alone in a car?" Mrs. Blatterman threw up her hands and spoke to the ceiling. "Will parents never learn? Every day, we hear of a child being abducted somewhere, and often it's because a parent left him alone, just for a minute, to run in and pick up a loaf of bread or the dry cleaning."

"I went to karate class," Lonnie Joe mumbled. "I figured I'd be laughed out of the gym if the guys saw me with an egg."

"*Maybe* you'll get a black belt in karate. You'll *definitely* get an F in child-rearing," said Mrs. Blatterman.

After class, I caught up with Lonnie Joe in the hall. My tongue felt like a slab of beef, but I managed to say, "I'm sorry about your egg."

"Don't be," he growled. "Only a dummy and a sissy would care about a stupid old egg."

He stalked away, while I stood there letting it sink in that I'd just been insulted.

"What's the matter?" asked Jiniwin, coming up behind me.

I started walking toward our lockers. "Nothing."

"Are you mad at Lonnie Joe? Did he do something?"

"Yeah. Today that creep lost a whole lot more than just his egg."

The bus was every bit as noisy as it had been the day before. Dallas was there, saving Reenie and me a seat in the third row.

"Hi, boy," she said as she scooted in beside him.

"Hi. And thanks," I said, sliding in.

"I got here early. Didn't want you girls to have to run the gauntlet." Dallas's ears lit up again, and I decided he was embarrassed by his chivalry. He was a strange one, all right.

When the bus pulled out, I searched my mind for a safe subject to talk about. Not school—where so many of the kids made fun of him. Not friends—I didn't know if he had any. Not family—he obviously wasn't close to his "old man." Definitely not pets—he might go off the deep end again if I mentioned Major D.

Reenie solved the problem. She stabbed a finger at the window and said, "Look, boy. My fire."

Dallas looked out at a man burning leaves in a ditch, then back at Reenie with a questioning glance.

"My sister's a bit of a firebug," I said. "She likes to watch things burn."

Dallas's eyes twinkled. "A bit of a firebug? Isn't that a contradictory statement?"

"I suppose it is," I admitted. "The truth is, she'd be a pyromaniac, except that we hide the matches and take all the knobs off the stove."

Dallas gave a rumbly, musical laugh that set me at ease. We were passing the fairgrounds, empty now on a weekday, and I asked, "What's it like at the flea market?"

"You've never been there?"

"No. My parents go sometimes. That's where Dad got his power saw—and our deep freeze. Mom came home mad as a wet hen about that."

"Mad? Why?"

"She said his dickering made them look stingy. The guy was asking only twenty dollars for the freezer, and Dad talked him down to seventeen."

Dallas laughed again. "That's the way a flea market works. The seller doesn't expect to get his first price, and the buyer doesn't expect to pay it."

"But how could the guy make a profit at seventeen dollars?"

"Maybe he paid only ten. Maybe he got it for free. But it's a cinch he didn't lose money. That's not how we operate."

I thought of how Dallas operated on trash day, how he towed that cart behind his bike, and suddenly I felt conspicuous at sharing his seat.

"You see," he went on, warming to his subject, "I pay three dollars a day for my space. If I sell twenty-five dollars' worth of stuff on a weekend, I clear nineteen dollars. That's all I need to—" His eyes clouded, and he clenched his hands. "That's all I need."

Need to what? I wondered, but I let it pass.

Fortunately, by then, Reenie was tired of being left out of the conversation. "See, boy," she said, thrusting a school paper into his lap and jabbing at it with her finger. "Star."

Dallas whistled. "Wow! A gold star."

"Four, five, s-six, s-seven . . ." With each word,

Reenie pointed to a number she'd circled in orange crayon.

"You're a smart girl, Reenie. That's a perfect paper."

Reenie slapped her chest. "Yeah, boy. S-smart."

"Reenie's not what you'd call modest," I said, grinning.

"Of course not. She's my best girl. And a firebug, at that."

"Yeah, boy," she said as she snatched her paper back from him.

When the bus was slowing at Dallas's stop, he said, "You girls'll be on your own tomorrow. It's Friday. I ride my bike to school."

Trash day. "Well, good luck at the flea market."

"Thanks. See you Monday." Dallas got off the bus and checked his mailbox.

" 'Bye, boy," Reenie hollered out the window. "Come to my house. Come to the farm."

THIRTEEN
The Trail

FRIDAY EVENING, Mom stitched curtains for the dining room and kitchen out of a set of flowered sheets. She was adjusting the last curtain on its rod when Paulette called and set it up for Jiniwin to spend the weekend at our house.

Mom gave an exasperated sigh when she hung up the phone. "I'll never understand Paulette—or Frank, either, for that matter," she said. "They brought Jiniwin into this world, then abandoned her when they grew tired of each other. Frank could call more, could have Jiniwin visit him in the summertime. Paulette could stay at home and show an interest once in a while, instead of finding every excuse in the world to stay gone. This weekend it's a business trip. I wish somebody would tell me what kind of 'business' a court reporter conducts on a weekend at a luxury resort. Paulette and Jiniwin hang their hats in a fine house with fine furnishings, but they don't really *live* there. They simply exist in an emotional wasteland."

Whoa. Mom was getting preachy. This was the woman who'd been bending over backward to accommodate Paulette for as long as I could remember. She must have had a rough day at the nursing home.

When Paulette and Jiniwin arrived Saturday morning, Reenie and I were by ourselves. Dad was doing a fix-it job in Turnback, and Mom and Jim Bob were at work.

Paulette came in sporting a studded jacket and jeans, suede boots, and a new bleach job. I thought of Mom in her white uniform, bathing patients, combing their hair, feeding those too feeble to help themselves.

Paulette stayed just long enough to make me mad. She went from room to room, giving our downstairs the once-over. The dining room didn't have furniture, but the sun was shining through the new curtains, lighting up the writing wall with a friendly glow. Still, all Paulette could say was, "Hmmm, how interesting."

It's more than interesting, I fumed inside. Mom's worked hard to make this . . . *quaint*.

After her mother left, Jiniwin said, "You'll have to excuse Paulette. This weekend at Whispering Pines is going to her head."

I nodded. Jiniwin couldn't help what her mother did.

She stepped over Reenie, who was watching cartoons, to set her VCR and a movie cartridge on the TV.

"What's the movie?" I asked.

"*The Dinosaurs Return.*"

"You and your monsters. No wonder you get scared when you're in your house alone."

She tossed her hair back. "Monsters are fake. It's the crazies with the chain saws that put the fear in me. Hey, I brought some chocolate squares and walnuts, so we can make those million-dollar brownies."

"Just what I need. Another million pounds."

"Give it a rest, Buddy. You're not all that big. In fact, I think you've slimmed down some around your middle."

"Really?"

"Really. Now do we play the gourmet or not?"

We mixed up the brownies, and I was careful to remove the burner knob after we'd melted the chocolate. While the brownies baked, we sat at the table and thumbed through Jiniwin's latest teen magazine. The warm chocolate smell in the kitchen was torture to me, but when I saw the sleek bodies of the models in the book, I vowed to eat only about ten cents' worth of Jiniwin's million-dollar recipe.

Reenie came in, saying, "Payno. My music." However, she noticed Jiniwin's suitcase and other belongings at the foot of the stairway and went over and picked up Jiniwin's denim purse.

"Be careful," said Jiniwin. "Groucho's in there."

"I careful," replied Reenie, hanging the strap over her shoulder as she started for the door.

I lifted the purse from her. "Can't take it outside."

"Give you a dollar."

"Not this time. If Groucho got broken, Jiniwin would cry."

Reenie thought about that. "Yeah-kay, s-sissy," she said, and went on outside. Twenty seconds later, she was banging ninety-to-nothing on the piano.

At lunchtime, we ate sandwiches and brownies in front of the TV. Although I allowed myself only one teeny brownie, I licked every trace of it off my fingers.

I knew Mom wouldn't approve of Reenie watching the movie, but that seemed like the best way to keep track of her. Besides, the show wasn't very scary. Dinosaurs frozen in a glacier for millions of years came back to life and terrorized a city. The earth trembled, people screamed, and buildings toppled, but the dinosaurs looked as fake as a three-dollar bill.

When the movie ended, I began gathering up dirty dishes.

Jiniwin stretched and yawned. "I'm about to fall asleep. Let's do something physical."

"Like what?" I asked.

"Like take a walk. Explore the countryside a little. How about it, Reenie? Want to go for a walk?"

"Yeah, Jivven."

"Good," said Jiniwin. "We'll take along some more brownies. Have a picnic in the woods."

I was outnumbered. I wrapped up two brownies for them and grabbed an apple for myself.

Jiniwin asked, "Should we take our babies with us?"

I looked at Miss Molly's basket, sitting next to Jiniwin's purse on the table. They'd be a whole lot safer here in the kitchen than outside. "I won't tell, if you won't."

"Tell who what?" replied Jiniwin, the picture of innocence, and she breezed out the door with Reenie.

On my way out, I glanced at the clock. Two-fifteen. If we were in Turnback, we'd probably be checking out the clothes in Marla's Boutique or having a Coke and a doughnut at the Soda Jerk. Well, maybe not a doughnut, I thought as I ran my hands around my waist.

The backyard looked bleak. There was the piano within reach of the back door, a sawhorse for Reenie to sit on, that crummy smokehouse, the stubble left after Dad had cut the weeds. Farther away, in the barn lot, something flapped ghostlike on the trash pile. A ragged curtain.

"You know what?" I said. "I really hate this place."

Jiniwin punched me playfully on the arm. "But you'll like walking in the woods."

"Don't bet on it. You know how I feel about snakes."

"I'll go in front, so they'll attack me first."

I rolled my eyes and spoke to the heavens. "The

girl's always got an argument. No wonder she's so good at speech and debate."

When we reached the trash pile, Jiniwin yanked off the curtain. "Remember Hansel and Gretel? They got lost in the woods. We'll make ourselves a trail to follow, so we can find our way back." She ripped off a piece of the fabric and handed me the rest, saying, "You tear. I'll tie."

We traipsed behind the barn and into the woods, and Jiniwin waded carelessly among weeds and rotting leaves to tie a rag to a branch or a bush every little bit. It struck me that for someone who was so scared to stay at home by herself, she was incredibly brave in the unknown.

The leaves crunched under our feet, briers tangled around our ankles, and cockleburs clung to our socks. Birds scolded us. Reenie laughed when a squirrel darted across our path and shinnied up a tree.

After a while, when Reenie started breathing hard, we sat on a fallen log to rest and eat.

I was munching on my apple when Jiniwin said, "Listen."

I listened. "I don't hear anything."

"Just be quiet for a minute."

I listened again. Leaves rustling. A crow cawing. Calves bawling in a distant field. A crackling snap as a flash of rusty orange shot out of a thicket and vanished. I think it was a fox.

"This is my pumpkin," said Jiniwin.

"What?"

She patted the decaying log. "I'm sitting on a pumpkin with my friends."

"But you can go back to your velvet cushion when the weekend's over. I'm stuck out here forever."

"At least you're not by yourself." Jiniwin slipped an arm around Reenie's shoulders. "You've got Reenie and your mom and dad and Jim Bob."

"Sometimes I'd rather not have Jim Bob."

"You wouldn't see it that way if he wasn't your brother. In my book, he's a hunk."

"A hunk of what?" I said, and we laughed.

When Reenie's breathing was back to normal, we walked on, climbed a hill, and found ourselves staring down at the steeply sloping banks of a pit filled with brown, stagnant water. A snake zigzagged across its surface. Cattails sprouted in the murk along the edges, pointing like spears toward the sky.

"That's one of those clay pits Dad told us about," I said, suddenly nervous about Reenie knowing it was here. "Let's go." Taking my sister's hand, I led her down the hill.

We followed a fence row and came upon a clearing and a house that had been gutted by fire. Through broken windows, we saw blackened timbers lying crisscross inside. The chimney had crumbled, and the roof around it was caved in.

"Creepy," said Jiniwin, stepping forward.

"Dangerous," I said, holding Reenie back.

"Let's peek in the windows. In town, they rope off burned houses, so you can't get up close."

"They do that for a reason," I said, but when Jiniwin set off on her expedition, I was curious enough to follow with Reenie.

Standing on the front porch, I smelled the acrid odor of wet sulfur and rot, like a burn barrel left in the rain. While Jiniwin peeped in the window, I held on to Reenie and stared out at the yard—rusting car parts, a battered truck sitting on concrete blocks, a weed-choked flower bed in an old tractor tire.

When Jiniwin moved on, Reenie and I looked in the window at a mass of springs and stuffing that once had been a couch. Blackened studs showed where walls had stood. A chunk of fallen wallboard, its flowered paper peeling and stained from smoke, lay against the remains of a television set.

"Mess," said Reenie.

"Big time. That's what happens when people play with matches."

"Yeah, s-sissy. My fire."

"You're hopeless. You know that? Let's find Jiniwin."

We went around the house, past a screened-in back porch, where a galvanized tub was hanging on the wall. The wringer on an old washing machine had melted into a glob, while a pair of trousers on a clothesline didn't even look scorched. Weird.

In the backyard, we passed an old-fashioned water

pump, and Reenie caught sight of a porch swing suspended from a metal framework. "S-swing," she squealed, breaking loose from me and running over to it. As she sat down and pushed off with her feet, the chains gave out an irritating screech. "My s-swing," she said happily.

I didn't answer. I was staring at a head bobbing in front of a large grassy mound. It was Jiniwin's head, and she was obviously standing in a hole. "Jiniwin?" I said, moving closer, and found her at the bottom of some steps that led to an underground door.

"This looks like a crypt," she said. "Think somebody's buried in there?"

"No, silly. It's a storm cellar. A lot of old houses have them."

"Yours doesn't."

I shrugged. "Can't have everything."

Grinning mischievously, she reached for the doorknob.

The hair raised on my arms as I envisioned unspeakable creatures rising from the grave. "Don't!" I cried. "That's like a cave. There could be bats and rats. Giant rats, not dinky little white ones like we have at school."

"Buddy, you're the biggest scaredy cat."

"Me? I've never barricaded *my* door with a dresser."

"Okay. You win," she said, coming up the steps. "It smells funny down there anyway. I've seen enough. Let's go back to your house."

But Reenie didn't want to go. "My s-swing," she said.

"We'll have Dad make you a better one. Just listen to the racket this one makes. It hurts my ears."

"My s-swing."

Eventually, I coaxed Reenie out of the swing, and we headed back the way we'd come. When we saw the first rags on our trail, I explained to her how they worked. She giggled at this new game. "My trail," she said, and played the spotter all the way home.

FOURTEEN
Monster

REENIE WAS POUNDING AWAY at the piano and singing, "My trail, my music, my farm," at the top of her lungs.

"I'm surprised that piano's not begging for mercy," said Jiniwin, up to her elbows in dishwater.

I rinsed a glass and placed it in the drainer. "Maybe it is, and we just can't hear it."

The grins froze on our faces when the noise out back stopped abruptly. I ran onto the porch to see what was wrong. Reenie was gone, her sawhorse tipped over.

Seconds later, she came bursting in the *front* door, her face white, her slanty eyes so big they looked almost round. "Monster," she declared.

"What?" I said.

"Where?" added Jiniwin.

Reenie turned, hunched her shoulders, and pointed a stubby finger at the backyard. "In the tree."

"There's no such thing as monsters," I said as I wiped my hands on my shirt.

"Yeah, is. Monster." Reenie plopped into a chair and stuck her thumb in her mouth.

I knelt in front of her. "Reenie, those dinosaurs weren't real. It was only a movie. Come back outside, and I'll show you there aren't any monsters."

"No," she said around the thumb. "Monster."

Worried, I glanced at Jiniwin. "I'm in big trouble with Mom."

"You give up too easy. Come on, Reenie. Let's all go out together. You can play us a song."

"No way. Monster."

"Okay, then. I'll play *you* a song." Jiniwin headed for the back porch, and as soon as Reenie heard the outer screen door squeak open, she began sobbing, "No, Jivven. Monster."

Jiniwin plunked away at "Chopsticks," the only song she knew, and Reenie kept crying until Jiniwin sauntered back into the kitchen.

"You're right," Jiniwin said to me. "You're in big trouble."

Half an hour later, when our folks came home, they found Reenie rolling cans like crazy, and Jiniwin and I sitting glumly at the table with our feet up.

"Hi, girls," Mom said as she hopped over a can to reach for a brownie. "How'd it go today?"

Catching sight of Mom's white nurse's shoes under the table, Reenie heaved herself up from the floor and said, "Monster."

The last can rolled beneath me with the rumble of impending doom, but all other movement in the kitchen stopped. Mom, Dad, and Jim Bob stood motionless, staring at Reenie, as if someone had pushed a "pause" button. The air was suddenly heavy with their combined scents—medicine, sweat, and car wax.

"What'd you say, hon?" Mom asked at last.

"Monster."

Mom carefully set the brownie back on the plate. "There's no such thing as monsters."

"Yeah, is. In the tree."

"Buddy," said Mom, still eyeing Reenie, "how'd she ever get an idea like that?"

"We watched a dinosaur movie," I mumbled. "It wasn't even scary."

Mom glared at me. "To you, maybe. Not to her."

Dad walked over to Reenie and hugged her to his side. "You disappoint me, Buddy. You know how impressionable your sister is."

"It was my fault," said Jiniwin. "I brought the movie."

I'd never seen my parents get mad at Jiniwin, so I was surprised when Mom told her, "You're like one of the family. You should know better, too."

A horrible silence filled the kitchen. I traced a worn spot in the linoleum with the toe of my tennis shoe.

After a minute or so, Dad said, "Irene, let's take

Reenie outside and show her there's nothing to fear."

But Reenie wouldn't go.

Dad tried coaxing and bribing and just plain ordering her outside. She wouldn't budge. He oiled the hinges on the door, thinking perhaps the squeak was scaring her. That didn't work, either.

Suddenly, I remembered how she'd liked the swing at that old house. "Maybe it would help if you fixed her a swing."

The whole time he was hanging the swing in the piano tree, Reenie watched from the window, crying for fear that the monster would get him.

Jiniwin and I took turns swinging, showing her how much fun it was. Still no luck. She cried for fear that the monster would get *us*.

When we gave up and returned to the kitchen, Mom was trying to calm my sister, and Dad was working on supper. He glanced pointedly at Reenie as he rolled a chicken leg in flour. "I just hope you girls are satisfied," he said, and he tossed the leg into hot grease.

By then, I felt like the scum of the earth. If Reenie never again played in the backyard, it would be all my fault. The big sister who had always protected her had let her down. With a crash.

After supper, I shampooed Reenie's hair and took her upstairs to comb out the tangles.

Jiniwin, sprawled across my bed, said listlessly, "I could kick myself for bringing that movie."

"I'm the one who let her watch it."

"Your folks are really ticked off. Maybe I should go home."

"You can't go home," I reminded her. "There's nobody there."

I woke up early Sunday morning, shivering because Jiniwin had all the covers. After pulling back my share, I slipped out of bed to use the bathroom.

At the top of the stairs, I caught a whiff of coffee and heard my parents' disgruntled voices in the kitchen. Certain that they were raking me over the coals about the monster, I stopped to listen. Dad muttered something about growing calluses on his behind from chauffering Mom and Jim Bob to work.

"James, you're doing what you can," said Mom. "Your odd jobs and your unemployment check—"

"Are not enough," Dad interrupted. "I think I have to take Joe Cagney up on his offer. With any luck, I'll have the pickup running by then."

"No," said Mom, her voice irritable. "That's not the answer."

When a chair raked back, I clumped noisily down the stairs so I wouldn't get caught lurking. My parents looked up at me with startled faces. Without thinking, I asked, point-blank, "Who's Joe Cagney?"

"Who's eavesdropping?" countered Mom.

"Why aren't you in bed?" asked Dad.

"Potty call."

"So answer it, and get on back upstairs."

I did, then lay in bed contemplating what little I'd

heard. Something heavy was going on. Who was this Cagney guy, and what was his offer? Mom had said that wasn't the answer. The answer to what? None of it made any sense.

I must have fallen asleep, because the next time I opened my eyes, the sun was shining. Jiniwin was asleep next to me, again hogging the covers, but Reenie's bed was empty.

I headed downstairs to check on my sister's whereabouts, and heard my parents arguing on the back porch. Dad was saying we needed a fire in the wood stove, and Mom was saying we didn't. Why would they get all bent out of shape over a simple thing like that? When we lived in town, they were always touching each other and smooching, but I hadn't seen them do that once since we'd moved. A scary thought struck me—that this house really was doing something to us. Maybe it was casting an evil spell.

I found Reenie sitting on the front porch steps in her pajamas, stroking Tripod. I couldn't figure her out. The front and backyards were just one big expanse, with no fences or shrubs as a barrier. If Reenie thought a monster might grab her in the backyard, why wouldn't she be afraid to go out front?

Her straight brown hair was tangled from sleep, and she looked small and defenseless, but I knew she had the power to cheer this family up. Her music was magic. "Hi," I said as I sat down beside her. "It's warmer out here than inside."

"Yeah, s-sissy."

"It's warm enough to swing."

"No. Monster."

"Mom and Dad are kind of grouchy this morning. They could use some happy songs."

"No, s-sissy. Monster. In the tree."

Totally baffled, I heaved a sigh and went back into the house.

Dad was in a bad mood at breakfast because the head nurse had scheduled Mom to work four to midnight on Sunday, and eight to four on Monday. He twiddled his fork and frowned at Mom. "That's almost back-to-back," he said. "Why doesn't that woman give you a little consideration?"

"I'm the newest employee."

"Well, why don't you stick up for yourself?" he grumbled, getting up to fill his coffee cup. "Make a few waves?"

"Low man on the totem pole doesn't get to choose," said Mom, and she laid down her toast and stopped eating.

During the drive to and from church, I could feel an undercurrent of uneasiness flowing between my parents.

Jiniwin sensed it, too. "Are James and Irene still mad about the monster?" she asked when we went upstairs to change clothes.

I told her about what I'd heard that morning, eavesdropping.

She nodded, sat on the bed, and began working a pink sock onto her slender foot.

I moved around to the other side, so I could change shirts without showing my flabby middle.

"That's how it started between Paulette and Frank," Jiniwin said as I slipped off one shirt and pulled on the other. "Arguing about the little things. Blowing up over nothing."

I felt suffocated for a moment with the shirt caught on my head. I yanked it down hard. "You're on the wrong track. It's nothing as serious as all that. We wouldn't have moved out here if my parents were getting ready to split."

"I hope you're right. It's terrible being a statistic."

Reenie ambled into our room, and I helped her change into play clothes. I heard Mom downstairs rattling pans in the kitchen, and through the window, I saw Dad going into the barn. That wasn't like him not to help Mom with cooking, especially when she had to go to work in a few hours.

"Look, Reenie," I said. "Dad's outside now. Bet he'd love it if you'd sing him a song."

"No, s-sissy. Monster."

Lifting the feather tree from the dresser, I said, "Don't you think this could use some more buttons?"

"Yeah, s-sissy."

"We'll have to fish around in the junk pile out back."

"No, s-sissy. Monster."

Reenie ended up with five more buttons, but I found them by pawing through the trash all by myself.

That evening, after supper, Reenie picked up Tripod and said to Jiniwin, "Posh."

"Give me a dollar."

My sister paid up with a rock, and Jiniwin dug around in her purse and came up with some hot-pink polish. She polished Tripod's nails first and was just finishing Reenie's when the phone rang.

Jim Bob answered it. After mouthing to Jiniwin that it was her mother, he spoke into the receiver, "You sound tired."

Paulette tired? From her weekend bash at Whispering Pines? Give me a break.

"I'll bring her home," said Jim Bob, nice as you please.

I knew he just wanted an excuse to cruise the streets of Turnback, and he proved it by dashing upstairs to primp and change his shirt.

Reenie and I helped Jiniwin round up her suitcase, VCR, and other paraphernalia and carry it out to the station wagon.

I tried the tailgate. "Locked," I said. "We'll have to wait for Jim Bob."

Reenie let Jiniwin's bag of dirty clothes fall to the ground. "Too haiby," she said, and perched herself on the rear bumper.

Down at the pond, bullfrogs were croaking and the

ducks were skimming across the water. The red-gold sun was disappearing at the very end of the road.

"My sun," said Reenie, as if that ball of fire had been put there just for her. "My sun. My birdies. My farm."

There was no mistaking her adoration for this place. If only she'd forget about the monster.

I glanced back at the house. The oval glass in the front door glowed like a burning eye.

"That's weird," said Jiniwin. "It looks like the house is on fire."

I elbowed her in the ribs and cut my eyes toward Reenie. "Don't be giving ideas to you-know-who. As bad as I hate this house, it's still better than living in the barn."

FIFTEEN
The Purse

"Reenie, you'll have to hold still if you want pong tails," I said. "It's hard to hit a moving target."

"Yeah, s-sissy," she replied, but she kept right on jiggling as she loaded rocks into the red yarn purse Aunt Sage had crocheted for her at Christmas.

When I finished with the pong tails, they were slightly off-center. I glanced at the clock. No time to do them over. It was only twenty minutes before the bus.

"Buddy, telephone," Dad hollered up the stairs. "It's Jiniwin, and she says it's urgent."

"On my way." I gathered up my school things and bounded down to the kitchen, where Jim Bob sat picking his teeth and burping. Gross. On the way to the phone, I dumped my books on the table, grabbed a piece of bacon, and crammed it in my mouth. "Hi, Jiniwin. What's up?"

"I left my purse at your house. Will you bring it to school?"

I scanned the kitchen. The only purse I saw was mine, next to Miss Molly's basket. Bending down, I looked beside the chair where Jiniwin had sat poshing. No denim purse. "Are you sure you left it here?"

"Well, yeah. Where else could it be?"

"Okay. I'll find it. 'Bye."

As I hung up the phone, Jim Bob asked, "What'd she lose?"

"Her purse.

Dad motioned to the scrambled eggs and bacon. "You girls better get to eating. I'll look around."

"Be careful if you see it," I said. "It's got Groucho in it."

Dad didn't find the purse. He even looked in the station wagon, but he came back empty-handed.

"Somebody frisk Reenie," I said, and made a mad dash through the house. No luck. By then, it was time to meet the bus, so I had to give up the search.

A few minutes later, I saw Dallas, standing by his mailbox in gray corduroy pants and a blue-and-gray sweatshirt. Not bad, if they hadn't been so wrinkled. The sleeves of his Windbreaker were tied around his waist.

"Hi, boy," said Reenie as he got on the bus and greeted us with a grin and a salute.

"Hi," I said.

He sat down with us. The earth and mustard smells were potent this morning, although his hair was clean and damp. The mustard was obviously coming from his lunch sack, but I was mystified by that scent of earth.

"Hey, Buddy," called Jim Bob from the back of the bus, "I didn't know you had a boyfriend."

I pretended I hadn't heard, but I felt myself blush. If my face was as red as Dallas's ears, one of us was bound to ignite.

Dallas reached into his pocket and pulled out a green rubber frog on a key ring. "Bought this for my best girl," he said, slipping the ring onto Reenie's finger.

"My froggie," she said.

I watched as she wiggled her hand to make the frog swing. "You bought it? You shouldn't have spent your money."

"What's one little quarter? I cleared thirty-eight dollars this weekend at the flea market."

My mouth fell open. I thought about the battered suitcase and the footstool. "What in the world did you sell?"

"Electrical wire, a magazine rack, old books, Avon bottles. There's this one lady, Maybelle Murphy, who's nuts about those bottles. Calls them her 'jewels in the sun.' Since she can't get to the flea market until Sunday afternoon, I go around early Saturday and buy up all the bottles, and she buys them from me. This weekend, I hit the jackpot. I found eight bottles for sixteen-fifty and sold them for five bucks apiece."

"You're kidding."

"Nope. Maybelle doesn't haggle over price. Just forks out five dollars for every bottle I can find. Says it's worth it to her for me to do the legwork. She has about three hundred jewels now, and a lot of them came from me."

"I can't believe it. There are hungry people, homeless people, and this Maybelle character spends a fortune on Avon bottles."

"Collectors don't even think about things like that. They just know what they want, and they have to have it. And believe me, some of them collect some pretty off-the-wall stuff. Barbed wire, gas station signs, clocks, lunch boxes. The older, the better."

I told him about Aunt Ruby's egg carton chandelier, pecan critters, and mouse-eaten postcards.

"Too bad about the postcards. They might be worth something if they were in good shape. As for the chandelier and the critters—well, there's a big difference between collectibles and junk. You have to know what to look for. Check this out." Dallas handed me a fat paperback titled *Lucy's Guide to Antiques and Collectibles*.

I flipped through it. An old tobacco can, undamaged, twenty-eight dollars. A cobalt blue medicine bottle, twenty-five dollars. "Aunt Ruby had a hoard of stuff," I said. "It's a shame she didn't collect anything valuable."

"Some people are just natural pack rats," Dallas replied.

We were passing the fairgrounds, deserted now except for a man and woman loading boxes into an over-the-cab camper on an old Ford truck.

"That's Lou and Marie," Dallas said. "They'll be heading to Florida in about three more weeks. The flea market closes at the end of October."

"Then you'll have weekends to yourself, to do what you want to do."

"No. You're wrong. That's when I'll have to do what I *don't* want."

"Which is what?"

Dallas's eyes burned into mine as he retrieved his book from my hands. "You ask too many questions."

Too many questions. What was that supposed to mean? I was just being friendly.

He tried to smooth things over, but I wasn't in the mood to talk to a chameleon, especially one with ears that would glow in the dark. For the rest of the ride, I concentrated on Miss Molly—refolding her blanket, fingering her hair.

I was still mad when the bus dropped off the elementary kids and let us off at the high school, and I shot ahead of Dallas on the sidewalk.

Jiniwin, her eyes all painted up, was laughing with Lonnie Joe Ross on the bench. Was she making a play for him, now that I'd crossed him off my list? I felt a little bit betrayed, considering that she knew he'd insulted me with that crack about the egg.

I fixed my gaze on the school and kept moving, but out of the corner of my eye, I could see Jiniwin running toward me.

"You must really be spaced out," she said when she caught up. "You didn't even see me back there on the bench. Did you find my purse?"

I stopped, and someone bumped into me from behind. "It wasn't at my house. Must be at yours."

"You're pulling my leg, right?"

"No, I'm not. Dad and I both looked, and we didn't find it."

"Buddy, that's not funny. Where is it? Has Jim Bob got it?"

"Oh, sure. Can't you just see Mr. Macho carrying your purse into the high school?"

Jiniwin's face turned pale. "You're serious, aren't you? You really haven't got it?"

"Honest."

"Then it's Reenie. She's got it."

"Reenie's got her own purse this morning."

"Then she's hidden mine somewhere in the house."

"Jiniwin Ingles, you know better than that. Reenie doesn't hide things. Besides, you had that purse last night when you carried your VCR outside."

"Reenie's sneaky. She's always making trades, leaving dollars whether somebody wants to trade or not."

This couldn't be happening. My best friend in the whole world was putting down my little sister. "That's not fair," I said. "You're the one who started her trading in the first place. 'Show me the dollar,' you've said a jillion times. How's she supposed to know when it's okay to trade and when it's not? But she didn't trade you this time. You know that. We were both with her right up until you left."

"But she's fast. Fast as a flash."

"She doesn't have your purse."

Jiniwin's nostrils flared, and a crazy picture of a palomino stomping whizzed through my brain. "We'll see about that," she said through clenched teeth. "I'll have Paulette run me out to your house tonight, and we'll find it."

"You and Paulette just stay away from our place. We don't roll out the welcome mat for people who turn up their piggy noses at what we've got."

"Piggy noses? So that's it. You're mad at Paulette for her attitude. I can't help it she's like that, any more than you could help your parents getting mad about the monster."

"I'm mad because you're accusing Reenie of something she didn't do."

"Look, Buddy, I don't care about the purse. Reenie can have it. I just want my egg, so I can bring my grade back up."

"How many times do I have to tell you?" I could feel the blood throbbing in my temples as I punched out the next words. "Reenie—didn't—take—your—purse."

"Yes, she did. I don't blame Reenie, because she doesn't know better. But I'm furious with you for lying about it." Jiniwin spun around and pranced away.

I watched her disappear into the building. I

couldn't believe it. First Dallas, and now Jiniwin, had pulled the chameleon trick before my very eyes.

My legs felt wobbly, my hands icy, my eyes hot. The ten-minute bell sounded, and I just stood there. What was the matter with Jiniwin, anyway? In eight years, we'd had a few minor squabbles, but this was our first major falling-out. And probably our last. I wouldn't be friends with anybody who mistreated Reenie.

"Buddy Richter, are you all right?"

I turned toward the voice. My vision was blurred, so I couldn't see who had spoken, but I could make out someone leaning out a window.

"Is something wrong?"

Everything was wrong. It's not every day you lose your best friend over an egg. Unable to speak, I shrugged and bent to pick up an imaginary object from the sidewalk. Only when tears dripped onto my tennis shoes did I realize I was crying. Wiping my face with the sleeve of my shirt, I changed directions and walked away from the school.

Our house in the subdivision didn't look lived-in yet. There were no curtains at the windows, no toys in the yard, no cars in the driveway. Seeing it that way made me feel sad, empty.

My tears were gone. I went around to the backyard, set my books and Miss Molly on the ground, then climbed up into the tree house. Lying on my back, I thought about Jiniwin. Maybe she and her mother had had a big fight. That was it. Jiniwin was angry at Paulette, and she was taking it out on me. Or, more specifically, she was taking it out on Reenie, through me.

She had no right making all those accusations about Reenie being sneaky and not knowing any better, and me lying. Lying! I never lied. I'd learned my lesson when I was four years old, the day I swiped a lollipop at the drugstore and told Mom the clerk gave it to me. She marched me right back to the counter and asked the clerk, while I stood there bawling my eyes out. I never lied or stole again. Those few minutes of guilt were enough for me.

Even now, skipping school for the first time in my life, I felt guilty, and I knew I'd have to confess to Mom. This day was stacking up to be a real prize.

I stared up at the bits of sky visible through the leaves. Could Reenie possibly have slipped away with Jiniwin's purse last night? No. The whole time we were waiting for Jim Bob, she'd been right there on the bumper. More than likely, Jiniwin would go home this afternoon and find that purse in the refrigerator or some other illogical spot.

"Buddy?"

The voice gave me a start. I rolled over and peeked down through a crack between the boards. On the ground below, peering up like a baby bird waiting for a worm, stood Aunt Sage.

"Buddy?" she said again.

"It's me."

"I thought that was you I saw go by a while ago. What are you doing up there?"

"Thinking."

"Thinking. Hmmm, seems to me that's what schools are for."

"I'm playing hooky, but you don't have to tell Mom. I'll tell her myself."

"I'm not worried about your mom. I'm worried about you. Come down and tell me what's bothering you."

"I can't."

"Why not?"

"You wouldn't understand."

"Hon, I've done a lot of living in eighty-four years. I've seen the Great Depression and two world wars. I've buried two babies that didn't live more than a day, and I've mourned a husband crushed to death by a tractor. I believe that makes me capable to understand most anything."

Pow. A stomach-punch. I couldn't say a word.

"I'm going home now to put the kettle on, and we'll have a cup of hot spiced tea. Slow as I am, you'd better give me a head start." Confident that I would follow, Aunt Sage turned and tottered away across the yard.

A few minutes later, I was sitting in her kitchen, surrounded by colorful crocheted doodads—butterflies on the curtains, hot pads on the stove, a doll whose skirt hid the detergent bottle, a chicken that covered the toaster. On the table, the scalloped edges of crocheted coasters peeked out from beneath two steaming mugs of tea.

Aunt Sage wrapped her spidery fingers around her mug, looked me in the eye, and said, "I'll be honest with you."

I held her gaze, expecting her to reveal some valuable truth.

"I crochet to keep my hands busy, and then I don't know what to do with all the stuff. This place looks like a yarn factory exploded."

I couldn't help it. I laughed.

"There now. That's more like it. A smile is so much better than a frown."

It was easy then to tell her what was wrong, and as I poured out all the details, I felt my spirits inching up.

When I was finished, Aunt Sage nodded. "I can't say what's wrong with Dallas, other than his alcoholic dad, but I know what's wrong with Jiniwin. My phone's been ringing off the hook this morning."

Off the hook. My eyes searched out the phone. The receiver was nestled in its cradle. At least once in a while Aunt Sage remembered to hang it up.

"Paulette Ingles came back from Whispering Pines with a diamond," she said. "She's going to marry that lawyer fellow."

So that was it. No wonder Jiniwin was upset. I almost felt sorry for her, and maybe I could forgive her, just this once.

I got up, set my mug in the sink, and hugged Aunt

Sage. "I guess I'll go back to school now and try to patch things up with Jiniwin. Thanks for listening."

"It's my pleasure, Buddy. I miss having you folks close by. Come back anytime to see me, except don't play hooky to do it."

I arrived at school near the end of second hour. Instead of going to the office for an admission slip, I hid in the rest room until the bell. When third hour rolled around, I went to class and watched the clock until lunchtime.

But Jiniwin didn't want to talk at lunch. She wouldn't look at me, even though I was sitting right across the table from her. She talked to Teresa and Debbie and Mary Jo, but I was a nonperson. Invisible. Finally, when she got up to dump her tray, I followed. "Jiniwin, Aunt Sage told me about your mom and Reginald. I'm sor—"

Jiniwin whirled around and shrieked, "That gossipy old woman! She's probably kept the phone lines hot. Don't believe a word she says."

I blinked and stepped back. "I just wanted to say I'm sorry."

"Oh, yeah? Well, you're gonna be a whole lot sorrier if you don't give me back my egg."

"I can't give it back if I don't have it."

"Check around," she yelled, right in my face. "Reenie's always nosing into things. She's probably found a dozen hiding places in that old house that you don't know about."

"Reenie doesn't 'nose,' " I yelled back. "She's curious. And you know she doesn't hide things. She'll show perfect strangers what's in her purse, for heaven's sake!"

"Yeah, and if they don't watch her, she'll give them a 'dollar' and slip off with whatever she wants."

"Girls, what's going on here?" It was the principal, arms crossed, frowning and blinking like a savage owl.

For the first time, I noticed the crowd. Half a dozen kids were standing near the trash can, eyeballing us. One of them was Lonnie Joe Ross.

Mr. Honeycutt blinked at Jiniwin, then at me. "Are you going to tell me what's going on, or do we have to settle this in my office?"

Lonnie Joe spoke up, "Jiniwin's mad 'cause Buddy's little sister stole her purse."

Stole? Is that what Jiniwin had told him on the bench this morning?

Mr. Honeycutt's grizzled eyebrows lifted. "Stole her purse?"

"She did not!" I cried. "Reenie didn't steal anything."

"It's not the purse I'm worried about, Mr. Honeycutt," Jiniwin said. "It's my egg."

"Your egg?"

"Yes, sir. For family living class."

Mr. Honeycutt nodded. "I see. Buddy, who is your little sister?"

I opened my mouth, but before I could get the

words out, Lonnie Joe said, "She's that retard over in elementary. The one who sucks on her thumb and walks like a duck."

I felt my brain exploding in my skull. I snatched the tray from his hands and slammed it to the floor. Milk and mixed vegetables splattered everywhere, and a fork vaulted into the cuff of Mr. Honeycutt's suit pants.

"Enough!" he growled, kicking the fork away and gripping my arm.

As he escorted me from the cafeteria, I looked back over my shoulder. Lonnie Joe was on his knees, wiping a mess off Jiniwin's shoes.

SIXTEEN
Punishment

DAD'S FACE SEEMED CARVED OF STONE, but when I confessed to dumping the tray, his eyes flickered with anger. "Garbage," he muttered, and I felt hot from head to toe at shaming him.

"In all directions," said Mr. Honeycutt. "I'll have to send these slacks to the cleaners."

Dad uncrossed his legs and leaned forward, gripping the arms of the chair. "I mean the way that boy referred to Reenie. That's garbage."

My heart leaped in my chest. He was on my side!

"See here, Mr. Richter. Are you defending Buddy's actions?"

"No, sir, not exactly. But you have to understand that for nine years, ever since Reenie was born, our family has been fighting ignorance. Reenie has been stared at, laughed at, ridiculed, and tormented, simply because she's different. Do you know Reenie, Mr. Honeycutt?"

"I've seen her a few times. Just last week, I was over at the elementary, and she invited me to your farm."

"Then you know how outgoing she is, how lovable. You'd think a child like that would be loved by everybody in return, but I'm afraid that's not the case. We see it all the time—prejudice against her in some form or another. Kids not wanting to stand in line beside her. Grown-ups staring at her in the supermarket. Teenagers calling her 'retard' on the bus."

"Still, that's no excuse for Buddy to lose control and dump a tray in the cafeteria."

"I'm sorry about the *tray,*" I said.

"But not about losing control?"

"No, sir, I'm not. If I'd had the chance, I'd have blacked both of Lonnie Joe's eyes."

"None of that. Not in my school. Fighting would have gotten you a three-day suspension."

"What's the punishment for slamming down a tray?" asked Dad.

"I'm taking into consideration that Buddy's never been in trouble before. She's not like some students who are in my office every other day for one reason or another—misbehaving or mouthing off or cutting class." Mr. Honeycutt looked at me. "By the way, I assume you have a good explanation for why you missed the first two hours this morning and didn't come to the office for an admission slip."

"What?" said Dad, turning to face me.

"I—I—was going to tell Mom. This morning was lousy, first on the bus and later when Jiniwin jumped me at school. I went to the tree house to think. Aunt Sage found me, and invited me to her house to talk." To Mr. Honeycutt, I said, "I'm sorry for not getting the pass, and I won't skip school again."

"Buddy, in thirty years at this job, I've heard that line a thousand times. Why should I believe you?"

"Because I never lie, Mr. Honeycutt."

He studied me for about fifteen seconds. I didn't flinch. Finally, he seemed satisfied, and he said to Dad, "Mr. Richter, I'm not unsympathetic to your family's problems, and I certainly will have a talk with our tactless Mr. Ross. I'd rather not have to punish Buddy at all, but too many students saw her behavior in the cafeteria, so I can't let her off scot-free. I'm sending her home for the rest of the day."

"Fair enough," said Dad, rising to shake the principal's hand.

"Mr. Honeycutt," I said, "what about your slacks? It'll cost to have them cleaned."

A smile almost touched his lips. "Don't worry about that. It's just one of the hazards of the job."

As Dad got out of the station wagon, he said, "I'll be out in the barn, working on the pickup. Holler at me around three, so I can go pick up Reenie. Can't have her riding alone on the bus."

"She'll be okay with Dallas."

"Are you sure?"

"I'm sure. Dallas'll protect her from the kids, and he'll scare off any monsters."

Dad grinned, but the grin didn't seem to fit his face. He stood staring down the road, his expression faraway, on another planet.

What was bothering him? I was certain it was Joe Cagney's offer, whatever that was, and not the monster. "Dad, is everything okay?"

"What? Oh, sure. I'll be in the barn."

I went inside, called the school, and left a message for Mrs. Houston to put Reenie on the bus. Then I tore the house apart, determined to prove once and for all that Miss Big Mouth Jiniwin Ingles didn't know what she was talking about. I searched every nook and cranny, and the only unexpected things I found were a dead mouse in a trap in the bathroom and a live one in the window seat.

The afternoon seemed to drag on forever. I baked a batch of oatmeal cookies and washed a load of towels, but my thoughts were going in all directions. Just where did Jiniwin get off, telling Lonnie Joe that Reenie *stole* her purse? And was Dallas hiding a deep, dark secret that turned him into a Doctor Jekyll at the drop of a hat?

I was heading for the clothesline with the towels when I heard the bus stop down at the cattle guard. I dropped the basket and hustled off to meet my sister.

From a distance, I saw that the sleeves of her jacket were tied around her waist, Dallas-style. When we met at the pond, I said, "Hi, how was school today?" then chuckled, because I sounded just like Mom.

"Hi, s-sissy. My froggie." Reenie pointed to the key ring dangling from the top buttonhole of her red shirt.

"Looks like Dallas fixed it so you wouldn't lose it."

"Off."

"It's safer where it's at."

"Off," she said again, so I removed the key ring.

While Reenie was snacking on cookies, Dad came into the kitchen and teased her as he scrubbed his greasy hands. At a quarter till four, he left to pick up Mom at the nursing home.

I wiped crumbs off Reenie's mouth with a damp cloth, and said, "I've got some towels to hang up. Want to go outside and swing? I'll push you high enough to touch the clouds."

She pulled away from me. "Monster."

"There is no monster, but if there was, I'd protect you."

"Monster," she said, getting down on all fours to drag Tripod out from under the wood stove.

I glanced at the gas range. No knobs. "All right. You play with Tripod."

"My kitty. My s-swing."

Shaking my head, I went out to hang up the clothes. Not five minutes later, I was back in the kitchen. Reenie was gone.

I called her name. No answer.

"Not again," I groaned. I looked upstairs and down, but she wasn't there.

Because of the monster, I knew she hadn't gone out the back door, and besides, I would have seen her anyway. I shot out the front door, and when I didn't spot her on the road, I ran around the house. Still, I didn't find her. Shielding my eyes, I scanned the barn lot, hoping she might have gotten brave enough to sift for buttons in the trash pile. A movement caught my eye, but it was only a flapping rag, caught on the lumber from the hog shed.

Why had we ever moved to this awful place in the middle of nowhere? The woods, the pond, that field behind the house—there were a dozen places Reenie could be, and not one of them safe. I swallowed hard, but I couldn't ease the panic that was rising in my throat.

SEVENTEEN

Dallas's Parlor

BE CALM, I told myself. Think.

Would Reenie have headed toward town? If so, and if she stayed on the road, Mom and Dad would meet her in a few minutes. If she'd turned right at the cattle guard, she'd be in that dark tunnel of trees. I didn't think she'd go that way.

Then, remembering our first night here, I sprinted across the lot and into the barn. I looked in all the stalls and even in the pickup. No Reenie. As I stood there feeling helpless, her words echoed in my head, "My kitty. My s-swing."

I had a hunch that she'd gone to the burned-out house to swing. I ran into the woods, following the rag trail, praying that Reenie had done the same, yet steered clear of the clay pit.

I was huffing and puffing when I charged up the mossy bank and looked down into the pit. Its muddy brown surface was calm, the spearlike cattails undisturbed.

I ran on, zigzagging from rag to rag. When I came upon the clearing and spotted a flash of red, I almost cried with joy. There was Reenie, stooping to pick up Tripod. She snagged him and carried him around the corner of the house.

Slower now, and wheezing, I trailed after her.

As I rounded the corner, the swing screeched under Reenie's weight, then clanked and groaned as she set it in motion, with Tripod clutched on her lap.

I blinked in disbelief at what happened next. Dallas appeared almost magically, and it took me a moment to realize he'd come up the steps of the storm cellar.

"Reenie?" he said.

"Hi, boy."

"What are you doing here?"

"S-swing."

"How'd you get here?"

"She got away from me," I called, walking toward them.

Dallas whirled around, his eyes wide with shock.

"She's faster than a speeding bul—" I stopped. He'd hidden his hand behind his back, but not before I'd seen what was in it. A half-eaten sandwich. All yellow inside. Mustard.

Dallas flung the sandwich into the weeds and demanded, "Why are you spying on me?"

"I'm not spying. I came to get my sister."

"S-swing," said Reenie, wanting some attention.

"Yes, Reenie, but you've got to stop taking off by yourself." To Dallas, I said, "She can disappear in the blink of an eye. Our brother calls her the Flash."

As if weighing my words, Dallas glanced from me to Reenie and back again. Finally, a smile played around the corners of his mouth. "The Flash?"

I nodded. "The Flash."

"And I suppose the cat's nickname is Lightning." Dallas reached to pet Tripod, but in that same instant, the cat arched his back and hissed. He leaped down and streaked across the yard after a raccoon that had come out of the storm cellar.

"Tripod!" I yelled.

"Major D!" yelled Dallas.

The raccoon raced into the woods, with Tripod in hot pursuit.

"Dallas, do something!" I shouted.

"Major D can take care of himself. He lives in the woods."

"But what about the cat?"

"He'll come back. He'll never catch Major D. Can a Piper Cub catch a Boeing seven-oh-seven?"

"I guess not," I said, grinning. I plopped down beside Reenie and studied Dallas. He was grinning now, too. I knew it was risky, but curiosity got the best of me, and I asked, "You want to tell me why you were eating a mustard sandwich in a cave with a raccoon?"

He turned away from my gaze. "No reason," he

mumbled. As he wiped his hand on his corduroy pants, something clicked in my brain. The smell of earth. The melted wringer on the back porch, near the trousers that weren't scorched. Those trousers had been gray corduroy. I felt cold all over as the horrible truth dawned on me. "Dallas," I croaked, "you're living in the storm cellar!"

Every ounce of blood drained from his face, so that his dark eyes looked like black holes. "You can't tell anyone, Buddy. *You can't.*"

"But how—why—where's your dad?"

"Gone, and good riddance. He's the one who did that," Dallas said, sweeping a hand toward the house.

"Your dad set fire to the house?"

"Yeah."

"On purpose?"

"I don't know. He was drunk and yelling when I went to bed. He was still drunk and yelling when I woke up and saw the flames. I tried to put them out, but he knocked me down. Said he wanted us both to die."

"But I—where is he now? Did he—die?"

Dallas snorted. "No. He drove off in his truck and never came back. He saw me grabbing stuff to save, so maybe he thinks I burned to death."

"That's terrible. The police, the fire department, didn't they—"

"Nobody saw the fire. Nobody reported it. I've been living in the cave since the house burned in April, and nobody knows. Nobody but you. And you've got to swear that you won't ever tell a soul."

"But you can't keep living there. You'll freeze when cold weather comes."

"I'll be all right, at least until after Christmas."

"After Christmas?"

"That's when the really bitter cold starts."

"What'll you do then?"

"I've got an aunt in Hanging Rock—my mother's sister. She runs a greenhouse. I'll tell her Dad's out of town, and ask to stay with her for a couple of months."

"Won't she figure out something's wrong when your dad doesn't call or anything?"

"Aunt Gracie never had any use for my old man, and after Mom died, she let him know he wasn't welcome in Hanging Rock."

"But what about your house? When she brings you home, she'll see it."

Dallas's eyes sparkled. "I can tell you don't know much about greenhouses. By the middle of February, Aunt Gracie'll be up to her eyeballs planting seedlings for the spring. By March, when she's transplanting them, she won't have time to think. She'll be more than happy if I find my own ride home."

"What's so bad about your aunt that you don't want to live with her all the time?"

"My aunt never married, never had kids. I stayed with her the summer after Mom died, and she nearly pampered me to death. I'm not a begonia to be coddled or a shrub to be clipped. I was twelve years old then, and I didn't have much choice. But now I'm fifteen, and I can make a living at the flea market."

I stared at Dallas, really seeing him for the first time. Here was a boy who was fiercely independent. Who didn't care what others said about him. Who was making his own way in a world where other teenagers worried about clothes and dates and winning the ball game on Friday night. Here was a boy who needed every dime he could scrape up, but who was always giving Reenie some little gift. Suddenly his clothes didn't look so wrinkled, and his ears didn't look so big.

"I—I—could I see—where you live?" I asked.

"Only if you promise not to tell."

"I promise. They can tie me on a rack and pour boiling oil over me, but my lips are sealed."

"Fair enough, but I have to warn you—it's not the Ritz."

Strange. Mom had said the same thing about Aunt Ruby's house.

I followed Dallas down the steps to the storm cellar, where a broom was propping the door open to let in light and air. A chill passed through me when I remembered the day Jiniwin had almost opened that door. What if we'd discovered Dallas's secret then? She'd have broadcast it at school.

Silently, we stepped into a dim room that smelled of

soap and earth and kerosene. The floor of the cellar was about five feet square, not counting the rough wooden shelves that lined the walls.

The room was divided in half diagonally by a cot too long to fit otherwise. Beside the cot sat a kerosene lamp and matches on an end table with charred legs. As I focused on the cot—covers spread neatly, sock monkey on the pillow—I felt embarrassed to be here, painfully conscious of Dallas's nearness in that small space.

"Mom made Munk a long time ago," he said, his red ears all but glowing as he picked up the creature made of gray work socks. "He's just for looks. I—uh—don't sleep with a toy."

"Monkey," said Reenie, brushing past me. When he handed the monkey to her, she clutched it to her chest and plopped down on the cot.

"Don't sit on—" I said, but Dallas interrupted, "It's fine. As you can see, there are no chairs in my parlor."

I grinned and took a closer look at his "parlor." One shelf held bread, crackers, peanut butter, mustard, and a few cans of vegetables and Vienna sausages. Others held clothing, kitchen items, a wash pan, toiletries, and books. One particular shelf brought a burning to my eyes—framed photographs, a needlepoint pillow, a China doll, a pearl-handled brush and mirror. I knew they'd belonged to Dallas's mother.

"See?" he said. "It's got all the comforts of home, except for plumbing and electricity."

And heat for the winter, and a father who cares. I swallowed hard.

"I get water from that pump in the yard. To heat it or to cook, I build a little fire outside, like a cowboy on the trail."

"At least a cowboy's got a horse to keep him company."

"And I've got Major D. Sometimes. If he's feeling sociable."

"This is all wrong, Dallas. You need somebody to look after you. If not your aunt, then maybe some agency could—"

"No!"

"But you—"

"An agency would put me in a foster home—*if* they could find one willing to take somebody almost grown. If not, they'd put me in an institution somewhere. One tiny room. A cell. Maybe even bars on the windows. At least here, I've got my own space. I can come and go as I please. I do what I want, when I want. Actually, it's been good for me."

"Good? How?"

"I've learned to take care of myself. I've learned how to manage money. I'm making higher grades now than I did when my old man was breathing down my neck."

"You've always been on the honor roll."

"I intend to graduate at the top of my class. For one thing, I want to prove that I can do it on my own. For another, the top dog gets all kinds of scholarships."

"You've already planned that far ahead? All the way to college?"

"You bet. Business administration. Someday I'm going to turn some little company somewhere into a conglomerate that will rival IBM."

I giggled. "Anybody who can sell Avon bottles for five dollars apiece already has a good start."

"Not Avon bottles—jewels. Jewels in the sun."

EIGHTEEN
Flags and Rotten Eggs

WHEN REENIE AND I EMERGED from the woods, we stopped in our tracks and stared at all the bright patches of color in the backyard. Strings of red, yellow, and blue triangular flags radiated out from the piano tree to the back porch, the smokehouse, and the fence, and Jim Bob was fastening a fourth string to the tractor.

"Flags, Jay-Bob?" called Reenie.

"Mort didn't need 'em at the car wash, so I brought 'em home for you."

"My flags."

"Come and sing me a song, and try out your new swing."

"No, Jay-Bob. Monster."

"Not with all these flags flying. Monsters don't like flags. Come on. Pretend you're an acrobat swinging on a trapeze."

"Monster," replied Reenie, taking my hand and pulling me toward the front of the house.

I glanced back over my shoulder at Jim Bob. He was standing dejectedly, frowning at the flags.

"My kitty!" exclaimed Reenie. "Come home!"

Sure enough, Tripod was waiting for us on the front porch. Reenie grabbed him up and buried her face in his fur. Since he was still in one piece, I supposed he hadn't caught up with Major D.

"I wondered where you were," said Mom, holding the screen door open for us. She hugged Reenie and asked me about my day.

"Didn't Dad tell you?"

"Yes, but I want to hear the details. Talk to me while I get the hamburgers on to cook."

We went into the kitchen. I washed my hands, then set the table and filled her in on the great purse fiasco.

She didn't say much during my story, but the hamburger patties got slapped around a lot. "It makes you wonder about people," she said as she slammed the last patty into the skillet. "Lonnie Joe's mother is a speech therapist at the Disabled Children Center, and his father's on the board. You'd think their son would have a little compassion."

I glanced at my sister, who was trying to hang her key-ring frog on top of the feather tree, like a star. "Some kids wouldn't know compassion if they fell over it. You'd be surprised at the ones who make fun of Reenie."

"No, I probably wouldn't," Mom said. "I once

knew a girl with spina bifida who came to school in a wheelchair. She had tiny feet and wore diapers, and the superintendent's daughter taunted her about it on the sly."

"Couldn't anybody stop her?"

"Nora was too slick to do it in front of the teachers. Some of us kids went to the school board, but that didn't help. The superintendent said we were jealous of Nora and making it all up."

"Weren't you furious?"

"Absolutely livid, but there was nothing we could do. Maybe I'd have gotten somebody's attention if I'd snatched Nora's tray in a crowded room and slammed it to the floor."

I stared at her, not comprehending, but I caught on when she started grinning. Mom was telling me it was okay about my tantrum in the cafeteria.

Pulling back the curtain, she said to Reenie, "Jim Bob sure has hung some fancy flags. Makes it just right for singing and swinging."

Reenie pretended not to hear.

"I'll do it," I said, winking at Mom and heading for the back door.

"No, s-sissy. Monster."

I gave up and went to the refrigerator for the pickles, ketchup, and mustard.

Mustard. I knew now that Dallas was forced to eat mustard sandwiches because he had no refrigeration. I frowned at the jar. Mustard wasn't that great, even on a hamburger. Didn't Dallas ever get tired of it? Or of crackers and peanut butter and plain old canned vegetables?

"She'll forget, eventually," Mom said.

"What?"

"Reenie'll forget about the monster."

I nodded, realizing Mom had misunderstood my frown. If I didn't want to betray Dallas, I'd have to be careful, even with my thoughts.

The phone rang while we were eating supper. It was Jiniwin's mother, and Mom was ready for her. "Paulette," she began patiently, "Buddy has searched this house over, and that purse isn't here."

Paulette's agitated voice carried across the kitchen, and I picked up parts of what she was saying. ". . . making excuses . . . potato chips right off the coffee table . . . failing grade . . . want it back."

Finally, Mom had had enough. "Paulette, in the twenty-odd years I've known you, you've been a master of excuses—why you didn't make queen in high school, why you couldn't stay married, why you couldn't get home to take care of your own daughter. Kids learn by example, so it's no surprise that Jiniwin's making excuses now. She lost her purse somewhere between our house and yours, and she's blaming Reenie. Can't you just hear it? The teacher says, 'So some little retarded girl stole your purse? That's too bad. I'll give you another chance.' "

". . . excuses yourself . . . holding up for her . . . *is* retarded . . . sneaky."

Mom slammed down the receiver and came back to the table. "I'm so mad, I'm shaking."

"At least Paulette got an earful," said Dad. "It's about time."

"I'll bet everybody in Turnback can hear her squawking," laughed Jim Bob. "I'm glad we're four miles away."

Later, I sat at the table doing homework, while my family watched a comedy on TV. Canned laughter, as if viewers wouldn't know when something was funny.

Miss Molly was eyeing me with her baby blues, and her hoop earrings gleamed in the light. I picked her up and blew on her plume of orange hair. The Magic Marker lines made her appear cracked, but she felt smooth as glass in my hand. Her looks were deceiving, I knew, because by now, she was rotten inside. It struck me that that's the way I felt about Jiniwin.

It was strange the way people and appearances could fool you. Take Dallas, for instance. He wasn't much to look at, but he was smart and strong-willed—and so kind to Reenie. What had made him that way? He had every reason to be bitter at the world. His mother was dead, his father a drunk, his home destroyed. He didn't even have any friends that I knew of.

And now I didn't, either. Acquaintances, yes, but no real friends. Jiniwin and I had been so close for so long, I hadn't cultivated other friendships.

"That's what happens," I murmured to Miss Molly, "when you put all your eggs in one basket."

Miss Molly just stared at me, looking cracked.

"The silent treatment. That's what I'll get from Jiniwin. Not that I want to hear anything she has to say anyway, unless it's an apology."

More canned laughter from the living room. I set Miss Molly back in her basket, gathered up my books, then went in to say good night.

"Are you sick?" Mom asked, because I never went to bed before Reenie.

"No. Just deathly sleepy."

As soon as my head hit the pillow, I was unconscious. But my sleep was filled with disturbing dreams, and when Jiniwin hurled a rotten egg at me, I awoke with a start. Reenie was snoring softly in her bed.

I pattered downstairs barefooted to use the bathroom. Although the kitchen was dark, a light was on in the living room. I heard Dad say, ". . . can't even afford health insurance, so what if Buddy or Jim Bob gets sick? Medicaid won't pay their bills."

"Then we'll deal with it," said Mom. "Don't worry so much. They're healthy kids, and if they should have an accident, they're covered by those policies we bought through the school."

"I'm tired of going one step forward and two steps back. There'll be bills for starting service on the phone and lights, and the charge for filling the propane tank just about wiped us out. I'm supposed to be the breadwinner, Irene. I've got to take that job. The pay is too good to pass up. Besides, it's only for three months."

I tiptoed over and peeked around the corner. Mom, in her nightgown, had wrapped herself in the granny-square afghan, and she was nestled up to Dad on the couch.

"Maybe you could find something closer," she said. "Maybe Kansas City. Then you could at least come home on weekends."

"Even the auto workers are laid off, and they're union. What chance would I have getting a job that paid enough to cover living expenses here and in the city?"

"But traveling all over the Midwest welding on tanks that have stored ammonia and fertilizers? The height and the fumes—it's dangerous."

Fumes? Dangerous? I shot into the living room. "Dad, you can't do it!"

My parents turned so quickly they bumped heads. "Buddy," Mom said, "what are you doing up?"

"I had a dream." I looked at Dad. "If you leave, I'll have nightmares. It's like Mom said. It's dangerous, welding on ammonia tanks. You could get blown to Kingdom Come."

"There are precautions—"

"Please, Dad. Do something else."

"I'm taking odd jobs. I'm even building a reputation as a handyman. But a man needs a regular paycheck to provide for his family."

"I'd rather have a dad odd-jobbing it than one who's blown to bits."

"Amen to that," said Mom.

"Come here, Buddy. Sit," said Dad, moving over.

I sat, and he drew me close to him. "I'm not gone yet. Joe Cagney is giving me a week to think about it. He has until the first of November to get a crew in place."

Three weeks, and then I might never see him again.

"I don't want to leave you girls," Dad said, hugging us close, "but we need the money bad."

I thought of Dallas, getting by on next to nothing. "Dad, it'll work out somehow. Money isn't everything."

But later, when I was back in bed, I thought about what I'd said. Money wasn't everything, but it *was* terribly important. If we had money, Dad wouldn't feel like he'd let the family down. Mom wouldn't be working that dead-end job at the nursing home. We'd still be in Turnback instead of in this rattletrap house. Jiniwin wouldn't have lost her egg, and we'd still be best friends.

NINETEEN
Sharing the Load

TUESDAY, knowing school would be the pits, I dreaded boarding the bus.

When Dallas got on, he showed Reenie a rock—mingled gray and white with one side mirror-shiny. "Found it down by the creek," he said.

"Dollar. Pretty dollar."

"I wish," he replied as he handed it to her.

She weighed it in her palm. "Haiby."

"It is heavy. It's galena. Contains lead."

Reenie squinted at the rock mirror.

"Oh, remember Munk?" said Dallas. "He says to tell you, 'Hi.' "

"Monkey." Reenie giggled and traced the shape of the rock with her finger.

"He was glad to see you yesterday. He doesn't get many visitors, except for Major D. By the way, how's Tripod? Did he make it home okay?"

"Yeah, boy."

"I think maybe that cat got your sister's tongue. She hasn't said a word since I got on the bus." When I still didn't say anything, he asked me, "Is something wrong?"

I shrugged. It didn't seem right for me to lay my problems on him when he had enough of his own.

"Half burden, double joy," he said.

"What?"

"It's something my mom used to say. It means sharing a load with a friend makes it easier to carry."

Dallas grinned at me, and I was struck by a revelation. He *was* a friend, and had been all along. I'd been too blind to see it, too concerned at what other kids would say, especially Jiniwin. I squirmed in my seat, recalling what he'd said once: "What matters is what I think of myself."

"To tell you the truth," he went on, "you halved my burden yesterday."

"I did?"

"Yeah. It feels good having someone to share my deep, dark secret with—as long as you don't tell."

"Boiling oil," I said, pretending to zip my lip.

He reached across Reenie and unzipped it. I think my mouth turned to stone. I couldn't speak. I couldn't breathe. Never had a boy touched my lips before.

Dallas's shadowy brown eyes were twinkling, and his ears were red. In that instant, I realized that the ears, all along, had been turning red for me. For Buddy Rae Richter, the milk carton with the Howdy

Doody hair. Not for Jiniwin Ingles, the beauty queen.

"Well, I'm waiting," Dallas said.

"W-w-waiting?"

"To halve your burden."

I licked my stony lips, swallowed, licked again. Stumbling over the words, I told Dallas what was bothering me.

He sympathized with me about Dad's possible welding job, and nodded wisely at the part about Jiniwin. "Doesn't surprise me," he said. "Alcohol can do strange things to the brain."

"Alcohol?" My voice came out in a squeal, so I tried again. "Alcohol?"

"Remember that Friday when I gave Reenie the sequin purse? While you were talking to me, Jiniwin hid a paper sack in somebody's trash can. I dug it out later and found an empty liquor bottle."

"Maybe you looked in the wrong trash can. Jiniwin wouldn't—she didn't—I know her better than anybody, and I've never seen her drink." But even as I spoke, I feared Dallas was right. Images of Jiniwin flashed through my brain. Her squawking fit over the See 'n' Say. Her painted eyes and the "shampoo" that made them red. She'd even slipped and told me about checking out the globe. And hadn't I suspected that strange smell in her room was wine? It certainly wasn't strawberry potpourri.

Dallas saw that I believed him. "I hope she gets help before it's too late, before she gets addicted." He wore such a scowl, I knew he was thinking about his father.

"Dallas, what should I do? If I tell, nobody'll believe me. Jiniwin will deny it, and everybody'll think I made up a story to get even with her."

Dallas didn't have an answer.

The bus stopped at the elementary, and I watched my sister being jostled along the aisle. Like Reenie, I had a monster of my own now—Jiniwin's drinking.

"Can't you tell your parents?" Dallas asked when the bus was moving again.

I thought about the big globe. Paulette had bought it after the divorce, and Mom and Dad didn't know it was a liquor cabinet. "I'm not even sure *they'd* believe me. They don't drink a drop, don't allow it in the house."

"Well, I'm all ears if you need to talk. Just remember—half burden, double joy."

I smiled halfheartedly about the ears, but as we got off the bus, my new knowledge about Jiniwin was a terrible burden. "Haiby," as Reenie would have said. Haiby as lead.

Inside the building, Dallas patted my shoulder and said, "Chin up, Buddy. It'll work out," before going on his way to the senior high.

The air was so thick with the smell of chili, I could practically see it boiling and bubbling in a cauldron. My stomach churned as I walked down the junior high hallway.

Jiniwin was taking books from her locker. She caught me looking at her, then turned away, but not before I saw she'd gone heavy on the eye paint. I pictured her hitting the bottle before school. Had she been building up courage to face me? The thought made me sad, but only for a moment. She'd cooked up that wild tale about Reenie, and she was asking for trouble by drinking.

All morning, my stomach roiled as the chili got more potent. When lunchtime rolled around, I couldn't have touched a bite of it.

Jiniwin beat me to the cafeteria and sat at our regular table with Teresa and Debbie and Mary Jo. That left me out in the cold. There I was, surrounded by a hundred kids, and I felt totally alone. After snatching up some milk and crackers, I slipped down the hall to the living lab with Miss Molly.

I set her on the ledge that ran in front of the cages. Precious was napping under his cedar chips, so I talked to Porky while I ate. "What's it like in Egypt, fella? Did you ever see a mummy or the Sphinx?"

Porky sat on his hind legs and licked his left front paw.

"Did you know those mummies are wrapped up tight and petrified? Like me. My hands are tied, my lips are mum, where Jiniwin is concerned."

Porky wasn't interested. He moved to a corner of his cage, leaving behind a trail of droppings.

Yuk. I threw away what was left of my milk and crackers, then killed some time by reading the printing on a feed sack. When I heard a rustling from the boa's cage, I turned around warily. The lid was in place, but I didn't like the look on Jake's face. He was staring at my egg with hungry eyes.

I snatched her up and fled, and we waited out the rest of lunch period in the girls' locker room.

After fourth-hour gym, I went to family living and sat at my desk beside Jiniwin. I might as well have been on Jupiter. She didn't acknowledge my presence, and I didn't hear one word Mrs. Blatterman said.

It was warm enough that Reenie and I carried our jackets as we walked up our lane. Yet smoke was spiraling from the chimney on the witch's head. The aroma wafting toward us was pungent and pleasant, not at all like the rancid odor of charred, damp wood at Dallas's house.

"Reenie," I said, "Dad's definitely rushing the season."

"Yeah, s-sissy."

Even with the windows and doors open, the house was hot. It smelled good, though, from the pot simmering on the wood stove.

"Yum," I said, lifting the lid and seeing ham and beans.

"That's how your grandma cooked beans when I was a kid," Dad said as he wiped sweat from his forehead with his shirt sleeve. "I'd forgotten how much heat these old stoves give out."

When Mom got home from work, she fanned her face, collapsed on a chair, and said grumpily, "James

Robert, this kitchen's too hot. You and that wood stove. You're like a little kid who can't wait until Christmas."

"Christmas. Goody, goody," piped Reenie as Dad escaped out the back door. She dragged a chair over in front of the dining room window, and placed her feather tree on it.

I shifted from one foot to the other, trying to decide whether or not to tell Mom Jiniwin's secret. Somehow, I couldn't quite get the words out. I guess a part of me was hoping it wasn't true. Another part was hoping Jiniwin would see the danger of booze and give it up without anyone else finding out.

Reenie walked up behind Mom and pulled the string of her See 'n' Say.

At the sound of crowing, Mom said crossly, "Hon, I'm not in the mood for that. Take it upstairs."

I blinked in surprise. Mom never lost her cool with Reenie. This was definitely not a good time for me to tell her anything.

Reenie tried to coax Tripod into the dining room, but since he was afraid of the See 'n' Say, he wouldn't go.

The phone rang, and Mom sighed, "I hope that's not for me."

It was, though. I handed the receiver to her, then went into the bathroom. Through the wall, I heard her saying that she'd lost a patient that day. Poor Mom. All the patients were her favorites, and she took it personally when somebody died.

My thoughts turned to Dallas. He'd seemed genuinely concerned that Dad might have to take a dangerous job away from home. And he was definitely interested in me. I stood before the mirror, studying my reflection and trying to see what Dallas saw when he looked at me. My face was ordinary. Blah. As usual, when my hair needed a trim, it was forming that Woody Woodpecker topknot. But haircuts cost money, and I knew we didn't have much. Maybe I could get by with a new style. I shampooed, wrapped my head in a towel, and headed upstairs to experiment with Jim Bob's blow dryer.

Ten minutes later, the dryer had fluffed me up like a brand-new dust mop. Disgusted, I hustled down to the bathroom, wet my hair, and slicked it back with a comb. When I went into the kitchen, Mom was just signing off on the phone. Outside, I heard a motor idling and Dad and Jim Bob congratulating themselves. They'd done it—gotten the pickup running. Did that put Dad one step closer to accepting the welding job?

As soon as supper was over, Dad jangled the truck keys at Mom. "How about if us mechanics take you ladies for a little spin? It'll be the countrified version of a ride around the horn."

Reenie dropped her fork and stood up eagerly. "Yeah, Dod. Horn."

"You don't mean in the truck?" said Mom. "We wouldn't all fit."

Dad slipped over behind her and nuzzled her neck. "In your younger days, Irene, you'd have jumped at the chance to be crammed in the cab of a pickup with me."

Mom blushed like a teenager. "Oh, all right. I'll go. Maybe it'll take my mind off things at work. Come on, girls."

The truck had rusted out around its fenders, the seat was torn and dirty, and where the shift lever should have been was a pair of locking pliers. But from the grins on Dad's and Jim Bob's faces, you'd have thought that truck was a limousine. We all climbed in—Dad in the driver's seat, Reenie on Mom's lap, and me on Jim Bob's.

Dad cranked up the engine. "It sounds good," he said, "but the shocks are bad. She rides rough as a lumber wagon." With a yank on the pliers, he found low gear, and we moved forward.

"I'm impressed," Mom said. "I wasn't sure this old crate would ever run at all, but you've got it purring like a kitten."

"That Jim Bob's turning out to be a real mechanic," Dad said.

My brother's response was a yowl of pain in my ear as we hit the bump at the cattle guard.

Dad steered to the right, into the tunnel of trees. "This rig brings back memories of my grandpa's," he said. "His old flivver was a disaster on wheels. The passenger door wouldn't latch, so he had to tie it shut with binder twine. Once, the bumper fell off and broke my big toe. . . ."

Dad told a couple of comical stories about his boyhood, stories we'd never heard before. Everyone laughed, but in the back of my mind was the worry that he was passing on these bits of history now because he might never have another chance.

We rode past woods and fields and farmhouses, bearing right at each crossroads until we came to the silo with the tree sticking out. Dad was making a circle, as he had so many times in the subdivision.

It wasn't the same. In Turnback Heights, we'd seen people trimming shrubs, sweeping sidewalks, playing badminton. Out here was nothing but cows, cows, and more cows.

When the truck bounced over the cattle guard, Jim Bob bawled like a calf in my ear.

"That hurts," I said. "Quit it."

"An elephant on your knees is what hurts," he whispered, pinching the flesh at my waist.

I gripped the dashboard and stared straight ahead. The witch's head was disguised by the gathering darkness, and the glow from the yard light showed smoke curling toward us. Someone had left the living room light on, so the oval front door glass and the windows on either side of it were bathing the front porch in yellow.

"Oh, look, James," breathed Mom. "I haven't seen this at dusk before. The house is welcoming us."

She wanted the place to be warm and friendly, and she was seeing things that weren't there. The house had cast a spell, all right—just not the way I'd expected.

TWENTY
Buttons

WEDNESDAY MORNING, Dallas had still another rock for Reenie. This one was brown with a hole in the center. It reminded me of the good-luck necklace Jiniwin's mother hadn't let her wear.

"It's a friendship rock," Dallas said. "The circle represents unending friendship."

"Yeah, boy. Dollar."

I smiled at him and felt a tingling clear down to my toes. Dallas was stealing my heart, just by being kind to Reenie. Maybe other people associated romance with flowers and chocolates, but to me it was the smell of clean earth and mustard.

When the bus stopped at the elementary school, Dallas caught Reenie's hand as she got up. "Friends forever?"

"Yeah, boy. My friend."

That day at school was just as bad as the one

before. I spent lunchtime thumbing through a magazine in the library, listening to my stomach growl, and thinking about Jiniwin. I'd noticed her cozying up to Bret Hopkins in the hall. Did that mean Lonnie Joe was already out of the picture?

Fifth hour, Mrs. Blatterman beamed at us. "Tomorrow's D-Day. I'm eager to see how you've changed your impressions about parenting."

I studied Jiniwin out of the corner of my eye. She was doodling on her notebook with a purple marker.

The teacher strolled around the room, looking at our eggs. I watched her every move, scared of what would happen when she got to us. Would Jiniwin announce to the whole class that Reenie was a thief?

Finally, Mrs. Blatterman stopped between our desks, blocking my view of Jiniwin, and asked, "Where's Groucho?"

Jiniwin spoke so softly, I barely heard her. "He had an accident."

"What do you mean—an accident?"

"A car accident," volunteered Lonnie Joe with a smirk.

"Turn around and mind your own business," snapped Mrs. Blatterman. "Jiniwin can speak for herself."

My brain was stalled back there on "accident." Somehow, Groucho had been found. Reenie was off the hook.

"I—I—Groucho was in my purse," said Jiniwin. "I must have left it on the roof of a car Sunday evening.

Somebody found it in a ditch along the highway and turned it in at the police station. I got it back last night."

"And Groucho was dead. Smashed to smithereens," said Lonnie Joe, his smirking face toward us again.

My brain was starting to process now. I saw Lonnie Joe's cold green eyes and the gap between his teeth, and I wondered how I'd ever thought he was cute.

Mrs. Blatterman said to Jiniwin, "I'll be speaking to your mother Friday during the parent-teacher conference. I'll have to tell her that you've failed your parenting project."

"She'll be out of town," mumbled Jiniwin. "She won't care, anyway."

"Of course, she'll care. That's what mothers do."

Jiniwin shook her head.

"Believe me, your mother cares. She didn't go off and leave you on the roof of a car, did she?" said Mrs. Blatterman, and she moved on up the aisle.

The rest of the hour, she lectured us on appreciating our parents. Jiniwin sat hunched over, while I stared off into space. It was the longest forty-three minutes of my life.

When the bell rang, Jiniwin escaped. She didn't say one word to me, or give me a chance to say anything to her.

So that's the way it was going to be. No note. No apology. No nothing.

No wonder. She'd made a federal case out of her missing purse, and now, to make things right, she'd have to eat crow. I cringed inside, praying she wouldn't wash it down with booze.

After supper, I sat at the kitchen table, reading. I was listening for the phone, willing it to ring, willing Jiniwin to call and say, "I'm sorry."

Soon, here came Reenie with the feather tree. She set it on the table, turned it 'round and 'round, and finally removed a china button printed with tiny blue-and-yellow flowers. With a pair of scissors, she tried unsuccessfully to cut the thread. "Can't," she said, giving me a woeful look.

"Leave the thread on, or the button won't hang."

"Off. Boy. My boy."

I understood then. This was to be a gift for Dallas. I snipped the thread.

"Here, boy," said Reenie, presenting the button to Dallas as soon as he got on the bus.

He thanked her, then did a double take. "Where'd she get this?"

"It was Aunt Ruby's," I said. "I told you she had piles of junk."

"This isn't junk."

Couldn't he see it was just a button? You could buy a whole card of them at the store for seventy-nine cents. Still, I decided to humor him, because he was

Dallas, and because he looked so vulnerable with a lock of damp hair falling into his face. "It's really pretty," I said.

"It's a collector's item. You've heard of tinkers who used to travel the countryside on foot? They mended pots and pans, and sold needles and fabric and calico buttons like these."

"Calico buttons?"

"Yes. They represent a part of Missouri history, because of all the wagon trains that passed through here going West. The calico pattern on the buttons matched the calico on the pioneer women's dresses. Maybe your Aunt Ruby hung on to this one because it came from a dress worn by one of your ancestors."

"I doubt it. That button is one of a kajillion that were stashed all over the house."

"You mean there are more like this?"

"Not just like that, no. As a matter of fact, I've seen maybe a hundred buttons, and no two of them are alike."

Dallas whistled. "Buddy, you could be sitting on a gold mine and not even know it."

I felt my heart rate quicken. "Why? You mean that button's valuable?"

"Probably worth about four dollars."

"Oh." Four dollars wouldn't even pay for a haircut.

"Some old buttons are worth less, but some are worth a lot more. Let's say their average value is twenty dollars apiece. Multiply that by one hundred buttons, and you're talking two thousand dollars."

I gaped at him.

"Now don't go counting chickens before they're hatched. Here," Dallas said, handing me a paperback book, "you can borrow this for reference. Look up some of your buttons and check the prices. Then you'll know whether to get excited or not."

I opened the book and scanned a page. A dime-sized brass button shaped like a running deer, one dollar. A black spider button, fifty cents. Not much of a gold mine. I swallowed my disappointment.

"There are a lot of those black glass buttons," said Dallas. "They're reproductions of the black jet buttons Queen Victoria wore after Prince Albert died. The common people went into mourning with the queen, but they couldn't afford the black jet."

"You know that? Off the top of your head?"

"I read collector books a lot, so I don't make the mistake of selling something valuable dirt cheap. Besides, buttons have an interesting history. They were made out of anything people could carve or drill into—seashells, coconut shells, pewter, you name it. There was even a wood from Brazil called vegetable ivory. It was a hard root that was used as ballast on ships. The sailors used to dump it overboard at the end of the voyage, until somebody discovered it was good for buttons. . . ."

By the time we got to school, I knew more about

buttons than the average person should ever have to know.

I wasn't surprised that Jiniwin was absent. It was D-Day, and she had nothing to show for it.

At lunchtime, I ate with Teresa and Debbie and Mary Jo, although I didn't have much to say to them. Jiniwin was the one who'd always kept the conversation going. Finally, I said to Teresa, "Only fourth hour to go, and then we're all done being mothers."

She glanced at her egg. "Yeah. I'm plenty sick of Abraham Lincoln. Can't wait to throw him in the trash."

"I feel sorry for Jiniwin," said Debbie.

"Me, too," said Teresa. "She really hates to get an F."

Debbie nodded. "That's bad enough, and then there's her mother. Half the time, the woman's gone, and when she's home, she's googly-eyed over that man of hers."

"Yeah, and it's rubbing off on Jiniwin," said Teresa. "She's chasing anything in pants, and she's gobbing on the makeup. She's starting to look cheap."

I suddenly felt terribly disloyal, listening to Debbie and Teresa talking about Jiniwin behind her back. Mary Jo must have felt uncomfortable, too. She stirred her vanilla pudding and didn't say anything.

Fifth hour, Mrs. Blatterman examined the eggs and gave us the count. Out of nineteen babies, one had disappeared, two had died, four had been physically abused, and twelve had managed to survive under the care of their eighth-grade parents.

Mrs. Blatterman strutted around the room like a pigeon on a roof. "I'll have good news for some of your parents tomorrow. Sixty-three percent—that's a higher success rate than I've ever had before."

I couldn't see that sixty-three percent was anything to brag about. If a family had ten children and lost four of them, nobody would be handing out medals.

The teacher made a ceremony out of disposing of the eggs. To the accompaniment of highbrow music on a tape player, she had us file past a decorated basket and lay our babies to rest. When Roy tossed Ziggy into the basket, he cracked a bunch of shells. A horrible smell permeated the classroom and seeped out into the hall, and within minutes, the whole school stank of rotten eggs.

"Hi, Reenie-Beenie," said Dallas, tousling her hair. "How's my girl?"

"Hands off."

"Sorry. I forgot." He slid into the seat and patted his pocket. "I've still got my button."

"Yeah, boy."

"It'll be a nice keepsake." He looked at me, and his ears turned red. "I won't sell it, you know."

"I didn't think you would."

"I—uh—everybody was talking about the rotten eggs this afternoon. Are you glad to be free of Miss Molly?"

"Actually, I miss her."

"A person gets used to having things a certain way. Believe it or not, I missed my old man for a while. The cave was deadly quiet, but now I'm used to it."

"What'll you do tomorrow about the parent-teacher conference? Someone might check up on you when your dad doesn't show."

"Nobody expects him to. He didn't go when he was home. Who's going for you guys? Your mom or your dad?"

"Mom'll have to take off work long enough to do it. Dad's got a welding job at Deepwater."

"Your dad found a job? That's great."

"Not too great. It's just for one day."

"Still, it's money in the bank. You make it while you can. That's why I'll be out tomorrow picking bones."

I winced. Even though I understood the necessity of Dallas's exploring other people's trash, I wished he wouldn't be so blunt.

Dallas saw my expression. "My work may not be glamorous, but it's honorable. I've told you before, it's not what other people think about me that's important. It's what I think of myself."

"I know."

He indicated the book he'd loaned me. "Since we're out of school tomorrow, you'll have time to read up on buttons."

I nodded. I wasn't especially interested, but I'd read up to please him.

When the bus stopped to let him off, he caught Reenie's hand. "Friends forever?"

"Yeah, boy. My friend."

Mom and I were fixing supper when we heard Reenie say to someone out front, "Come to my house. Come to the farm."

Since Dad and Jim Bob were tinkering with the pickup in the barn, Mom looked at me, puzzled. "Who's she talking to?"

"Beats me." I laid down the spatula and went to the living room, where I spotted my sister on the front porch. "Reenie, who's out there?"

"My boy."

I pushed open the door and stepped outside. Dallas was standing in the shadows under the tulip tree. "Dallas?"

He waved at me. "Reenie came over to swing. I was just bringing her home."

"Well, you don't have to run off. Come on in the house."

"No, thanks. I'd better head on back."

"Who is it, Buddy?" Mom asked as she came onto the porch.

"It's Dallas Benge. Reenie went over to his place, and he brought her back."

"Reenie," Mom said, "what am I going to do with you if you keep running off?"

Reenie grinned and stuck her thumb in her mouth.

Shaking her head, Mom spoke to Dallas. "I'm forgetting my manners. It's nice to meet you. Won't you stay and have supper with us?"

"Oh, no. Thanks anyway."

"Have you eaten?"

"Not yet."

"Then I insist. Come on in. It's a way to thank you for returning my wayward daughter."

Dallas still seemed hesitant, so I threw in the clincher. "We're having chicken and coleslaw and corn fritters, deep fried."

"When you twist my arm like that, how can I resist?"

As soon as we were inside, Reenie took Dallas by the hand and gave him a grand tour of the house, while Mom and I went back to work in the kitchen. Mom was frying corn fritters and I was grating cabbage for the coleslaw, when we heard them laughing upstairs.

"Reenie loves this place so much," Mom said, "I can't understand why she has such a wanderlust."

"Dallas has a swing."

"So does she, and she's never used it."

Because of the monster, I thought, as guilt niggled at me.

"I was hoping moving to the country would help the situation," Mom went on, "but it didn't change a thing."

Soon she went out to the barn to tell Dad and Jim Bob supper was ready, and I hollered upstairs for Reenie and Dallas.

When Dallas came down, he pointed to the dining room, which still didn't have any furniture, except for the chair holding Reenie's tree. "Where'd you get the tree?"

"It's more of Aunt Ruby's junk."

"Maybe not. It could be an antique German feather tree. I'll pick up a book at the library tomorrow. There are lots of imitations on the market, so don't get your hopes up."

No chance of that. I didn't have any more hope in the feather tree than I did in those fifty-cent buttons.

My parents' steady conversation at supper was meant to make Dallas feel welcome, but it worked just the opposite. He was ill at ease, and careful with every response, so he wouldn't let anything slip. As soon as the meal was over, he thanked Mom and asked to be excused.

"It'll be pitch dark in the woods," said Jim Bob. "I'll run you home in the pickup."

"No!" replied Dallas.

Everyone gawked at him.

He ran a hand across his mouth and glanced around the table. His gaze settled on Jim Bob. "I'm sorry. I sounded ungrateful. But my dad drinks a lot, and it'd be better if you stayed away from our place."

"No problem," said Jim Bob. "I just wanted to show you my wheels. I'll do it some other time."

TWENTY-ONE
Hero

MOM SHOOK MY SHOULDER GENTLY. "Buddy, wake up."

I opened my eyes to slits. By the dim light from the hallway, she looked ghostly in her white uniform.

"We're leaving now," she said.

"Mmm-kay."

"Jim Bob's going with Dad to Deepwater. I'm off to the nursing home, and this afternoon I'll be at the parent-teacher conference."

"Mmm-kay."

"You'll have to get up," Mom persisted, "so you can watch Reenie."

I forced one eye open wide enough to see my sister's bed. "She's still asleep."

"I know, but I want you up before she gets up. Can't have her taking off someplace. Come on now. Rise and shine."

"I'll rise," I mumbled, "but I won't shine." Eyes closed, I sat up and wobbled on the edge of the bed.

Mom kissed my forehead. "Gotta run. Call me if you have any problems. I'll call you on my break."

She left me, and I sat in the dark and listened to the thumps from downstairs, the closing of car doors outside, the rumbles of engines starting. Muffled sounds. Comfortable sounds. Dreamy sounds. . . .

The next thing I knew, it was broad daylight, and Reenie was pounding on my back. "Monster! Monster! Up!" she cried.

"What?" I sat up, rubbing my eyes and blinking hard, aware of an irritating squawking somewhere close.

"Monster!" Reenie pointed to the window, her slanty eyes round with fear.

I stumbled across the room and peered outside, half expecting to see King Kong. A blue jay was squawking and scolding, fluttering from branch to branch of the piano tree. "It's only a bird," I said. "A noisy bird." But as I spoke, a limb dipped and the jay flew away.

My mouth dropped open. Wrapped around the limb, not three feet from my face, was a blacksnake as big around as a baseball bat. I saw an eye like a black marble, and a darting forked tongue.

"Monster," said Reenie in an I-told-you-so voice.

I tore my eyes away from the snake and stared at her. She was twisting the tail of her nightgown and sucking on her thumb.

"Off," she said.

"Reenie, I can't. It's a snake. I—I—I can't."

"Off."

I looked away from that trusting face, still pink and puffy from sleep. I'd always been her hero. She'd depended on me to doctor her hurts, protect her, but I couldn't help her now. Shivering, I ventured a glance out the window again. Was that the granddaddy snake Dad had herded into the field?

Suddenly, I was furious with my father for not killing it when he had the chance. Oh, how I hated this house, this property, this . . . snake pit.

"My s-sissy. Off."

"Reenie, I can't."

In my head danced a phrase I'd heard during the Olympics: "Our heroes may not always conquer, but they will forever try."

You're her hero. *You* can try, said my conscience. *You can do anything, if you set your mind to it.* I looked at Reenie again. Still trusting. Still expecting her big sissy to control the situation.

I turned and stared at the snake. Gulping in deep breaths of air, I tried to summon up my courage. Somehow, some way, I had to get rid of that creature. If I didn't, it would escape and haunt Reenie and me for the rest of our days.

"You stay here, where it's safe," I said at last, slipping my feet into my shoes.

"Yeah-kay, s-sissy."

Reluctant as a condemned man on his way to the

electric chair, I made my way downstairs, stopped by the bathroom for a potty break, then headed for the snake catcher on the back porch.

As I stared at the contraption, I wished fervently that it was half a mile long. I removed it and tried it out on the mop. It worked, but I didn't fool myself. An angry snake wouldn't hold still and wait to be captured.

My heart was pounding as I crept out the back door. All around me, Reenie's red, yellow, and blue plastic flags were flapping and snapping in the breeze. I focused my gaze on the tree. Its swaying leaves created a rustling noise that sounded like hissing to me. I couldn't see the snake. Part of me hoped it was gone, and part of me wanted to find it and beat it to a pulp.

Cautiously, I climbed onto the sawhorse, then the piano, and broke out in goose bumps as leaves brushed the back of my neck.

The snake had moved down the limb, but not nearly low enough for me to reach it. I worked the snake stick up through the branches, then stepped onto the fork of the tree and inched my way up. I had to do this just right—capture the snake before it got mad, so it wouldn't attack.

With my eyes riveted on my prey, I made a wrong move. The stick jabbed at a branch, which in turn jabbed the snake. Instantly, the creature's head snapped up, and its tail lashed at the limb. I drew back so fast, my right foot slipped and I almost dropped the stick.

I can't do this, I cried silently. I'm crazy for trying.

But the snake, on the defensive now, was coming after me, oozing down the limb like black grease.

Bracing my back against a fork of the tree, I positioned the stick with my right hand and took hold of the cord with my left. The noose was ready. I wasn't. My palms were sweaty, my pajama shirt cold and wet against my back.

The snake kept slithering downward with that fast, fluid motion. I imagined its shiny body coiling around my neck. I couldn't breathe. A darting tongue and two black marbles were coming at me. Closer. Closer.

Yank! I caught the snake!

In a flash, the reptile coiled itself around the broomstick. Its mouth opened and closed convulsively, and as its tail whipped back and forth, I teetered from the shifting weight. Still, I held on with both hands, too terrified to let go.

Feeling my way with my feet, I backed down from the tree, dragging the snake along with me.

I found the piano, the sawhorse, and finally, solid ground.

But I didn't have the slightest idea what my next move would be. What do you do with a snake on a stick? If you let go of the cord and slacken the noose, you're going to get bit. If you drop the stick and run, you're going to lose your snake.

As the creature thrashed, I glanced around wildly, searching for a place to dispose of it. The smokehouse was too dilapidated, too insecure. The barn. I'd haul the snake to the barn and throw it in the cab of the pickup. I laughed hysterically, remembering that's what Dallas had done with Major D.

My laughter died when I remembered the pickup wasn't in the barn. Dad and Jim Bob had taken it to Deepwater.

What then? I couldn't stand here all day, wrestling a snake. I couldn't stand here much longer, period. My shoulders and arms ached. The cord and the stick were cutting into my fingers.

I searched my memory, recalling the inside of the barn. Stalls, a corn crib, ancient machinery . . . a big, empty oil drum by the door.

"Reenie!" I screamed at the top of my voice. "Come down here! I need your help!"

"Monster," she said, so near that I jumped. I turned and saw her watching me from the back porch, her nose mashed against the screen.

"I'm gonna drag this thing to the barn and throw it in a barrel. I need you to get that piece of tin that's leaning against the smokehouse. Bring it to the barn."

"Monster."

"It can't hurt you now. Please, Reenie. My arms are getting tired. I need your help. Come out and get the tin."

An inch at a time, the screen door opened. Reenie stepped out in her fuzzy slippers, her eyes on the snake.

"Good girl. Get the tin, but be careful. The edges might be sharp."

Eyeing the snake over her shoulder, Reenie scurried to the smokehouse and grabbed the sheet of corrugated tin. "Too haiby," she said, but she worked hard, tongue hanging out, as we dragged our burdens to the barn.

"Lean the tin against the barrel. Good. Now you can go back to the house."

Reenie vanished like smoke.

I stuck the snake catcher in the barrel and loosened my grip on the cord. As the snake's head slipped out of the noose, I slammed the stick hard against the bottom of the barrel. Once, twice, three times. Finally, the snake uncoiled from the stick. I tossed the stick aside, slapped the tin onto the barrel, and piled some old tools on top.

Then I collapsed against the doorpost and shook so hard my teeth rattled.

A chord rang out from the piano, and another and another, telling me that, once again, all was right with Reenie's world. "No monster," she sang. "My s-sissy. My girl."

She was proud of me, but not nearly as proud as I was of her for fetching that tin. She had overcome her fear of the monster to protect me.

TWENTY-TWO
Grapefruit and Wrath

I THOUGHT ABOUT KILLING THE SNAKE, but I just couldn't do it.

When Mom called on her break, I was still weak in the knees, but I didn't mention our adventure. I wanted to see the look on her face when I showed her the snake in the barrel.

After Reenie and I got dressed, she played with the See 'n' Say while I fixed our eggs and bacon, and Tripod hid under the wood stove.

By nine-thirty, I had cleaned up the kitchen. Reenie was back outside, banging on the piano, with the cat curled up at her feet.

"My s-sissy," she sang. "No monster."

Smiling to myself, I went into the dining room and inscribed on the writing wall: "October 14, Reenie and Buddy capture monster snake."

As I turned away, a rhinestone button on the

feather tree glimmered in the sunlight, reminding me of a rhinestone pin Aunt Ruby had worn. My mind flashed back to a Thanksgiving long ago, when a dozen members of the family had sat here feasting at a round oak table. I could almost smell the turkey and mince pies. I could almost hear the laughter when Great-grandfather Richter lost his false teeth in the gravy.

Next month, we'd again be gathering with relatives, maybe not here, but somewhere. What would Dallas do on Thanksgiving? Would he have dinner at his aunt's house in Hanging Rock, or would he eat Vienna sausages alone in his storm cellar?

Dallas. How my opinion of him had changed. In fact, my whole life had changed drastically since last weekend. I'd learned Dallas's secret—and Jiniwin's. I'd gained one friend and lost another.

The truth was, I missed Jiniwin terribly. I was tempted to call her and tell her that Reenie really had seen a "monster," that the dinosaur movie had nothing to do with it. But I couldn't. She'd made those false accusations. Let her call me.

When the phone rang, I snatched it up. "Hello?"

"Hi, Buddy," said Aunt Sage. "Just checking to see if everybody's okay."

"We're fine. How about you?"

"Fair to middling. My arthritis is acting up. That's a sign the weather's going to change."

I glanced at the sunlight streaming through the window. "It looks good now. Warm and sunny."

"Not for long. Old Arthur Ritis hasn't fooled me yet. It's gonna turn cold and nasty. Mark my word."

"Aunt Sage, do you—uh—have you seen Jiniwin?"

"No, but she never came to my house, unless she was with you. Since you're asking me about her, I guess you didn't bury the hatchet."

"No."

"You young people can be awful stubborn."

More stubborn than an eighty-four-year-old woman bumping a ladder down the steps in her quest for the morning paper?

"When you reach my age," Aunt Sage went on, "you think about meeting your Maker, and you pay more attention to His Word. In the Bible, it says, 'Let not the sun go down upon your wrath.' "

I counted up. It was Friday. Since Monday, four suns had gone down upon my wrath. Four days without my best friend.

"Tell Reenie I'm crocheting a winter cap for her. Red with a white tassel."

"I'll tell her."

"And think about your wrath."

When our conversation ended, I stood still, thinking. I pictured Jiniwin and me braving the first day of kindergarten together. I saw us in the tree house, sending secret messages with the pulley. I saw her poshing Reenie's fingernails with hot-pink polish.

I saw her painted face, her nostrils flared with anger.

But then her voice echoed in my mind: "You'll have

to excuse Paulette. This weekend at Whispering Pines is going to her head."

When Paulette came back from that resort with a diamond, she'd shattered Jiniwin's hopes of ever having her parents together again. I tried to put myself in Jiniwin's place. How would I feel if my parents split, if one of them found another mate?

I'd be angry at the world, just like Jiniwin, and I'd probably lash out at anyone and everyone—even my best friend.

I dialed her number. It rang nine times before she answered in a strange, faraway voice.

"Jiniwin, are you sick?"

"Who is this? Buddy? Why are you calling me?" Her speech was slurred. Was it from sleep or from drinking?

"I just—I wanted to—uh—tell you I'm sorry about your F, and that it's all right about the purse."

"No, it's not all right. I feel like slime." Jiniwin's voice broke. "I'm just like all the other slimeballs who mistreat Reenie."

"No, you're not. Don't cry. This one time was a mistake. Forget it. Think about all the times you've been good to her, stood up for her."

"Your mom and dad must hate me."

"Nobody hates you. My family's not the hating type."

"Oh, Buddy, I know that. You're so lucky. I'd give anything to have a family like yours."

When pigs fly, I'd thought once. Now I knew she meant it.

Jiniwin snuffled. "Paulette and Loverboy went out dancing last night. I was scared the whole time, and when she came home in the wee hours, I freaked out. I thought somebody was breaking in."

"Were you drinking last night?"

Silence filled the line. Finally, Jiniwin murmured, "How'd you know that?"

"Dallas told me."

"Dallas? How'd he know?"

"He saw you hide a bottle in the trash. How long have you been drinking on the sly?"

"I don't know. A month maybe. Lately I can't go to sleep without a drink. It's my security blanket."

"How secure would you be if the house caught on fire and you couldn't wake up?"

"I don't drink much. I can handle it."

"You're fooling yourself. I'll bet you've already been at the globe this morning."

"Well, yes, but—I have to. Paulette left again, and it's so quiet around here, and lonesome. I miss you."

I felt guilty then, although, deep down, I knew her drinking wasn't my fault. I wanted to suggest she ride her bike out to my house, but I didn't dare. With alcohol in her system, she might end up like Groucho—smashed in a ditch. "You've got to talk to Paulette. Tell her what you're doing, and why."

"Get serious. She's lovesick. She doesn't even know I'm alive."

"You've got to talk to somebody."

"I have. I've talked to Jake and Goomer and Porky and Precious. They're good listeners, but they don't have any answers."

"How about Mrs. Royal, or the school counselor?"

"I can't. They're practically strangers. They wouldn't understand."

"How about Mom and Dad?" This was desperation speaking—I hadn't yet been able to tell Mom and Dad myself.

"The teetotalers? No way."

"Well, you've got to do something, before you ruin your whole life."

"What kind of life do I have, if nobody cares?"

"I care."

"Kool-Aid," said Reenie, coming in the back door.

"Hold on a minute, Jiniwin." I motioned to my sister. "Come here, Reenie. Talk to Jiniwin. Tell her you're her friend."

Reenie rarely talked on the phone. She didn't even take hold of the receiver as she leaned toward the mouthpiece and said in her gruff little voice, "Hi, Jivven. Come to my house. Come to the farm. No monster." Then, smiling at me, she said again, "Kool-Aid."

"No monster?" asked Jiniwin when I got back on the line.

I explained about the snake, and she gave a little laugh that turned into a sob. "I'm glad she still loves me. I love her, too, like a sister."

After that, Jiniwin couldn't seem to stop crying. We signed off with a promise to talk later, and I stood staring blankly at nothing.

"Gone," said Reenie.

I blinked at her. She was holding up the empty Kool-Aid pitcher.

"Gone," she said again.

"I can fix *your* drinking problem. I wish I could fix Jiniwin's."

I mixed up some cherry Kool-Aid and poured a glass for Reenie. We sat down, and Tripod jumped onto her lap. I knew he wouldn't have done that if he'd seen the See 'n' Say on the table.

"You were really brave today," I said as Reenie took a drink. "You helped me catch the monster."

Her grin was exaggerated by a red Kool-Aid mustache. "No monster," she said, reaching over and pulling the string of the See 'n' Say.

"This is a horse—" began the mechanical voice, and the cat dived under the wood stove.

The phone rang again. It was Aunt Sage. "Buddy, my nephew's coming to take me to Jeff City," she said, sounding less chipper than she had a few minutes before. "Didn't want you folks worrying if you called and got no answer."

"Is something wrong?"

"My sister—she's sick."

"I'm sorry. I hope she'll be okay."

"Thank you, hon, but it doesn't sound good. She's old, older than me. Rosemary and I were—are—so close. If this is the end, I just hope she doesn't suffer long. I'll call if—I'll call in a day or two and let you know what's what. I'd better get my things packed now. 'Bye."

" 'Bye. . . . Oh, Aunt Sage?" I intended to tell her today's sun wouldn't go down upon my wrath, but she was gone and the line was open. Although I whistled and yelled, I couldn't make her hear me.

"S-sissy?" said Reenie, confused by all my racket.

"Aunt Sage forgot to hang up again. It's a good thing Mom's got a key to her house."

"Yeah, s-sissy."

Listlessly, I picked up Mom's nail file from the windowsill and sat at the table to whittle at my nails. Reenie went back to playing with the See 'n' Say, and by the time I'd listened to a dog, a turkey, a cow, and a duck, I was ready to join Tripod under the stove.

"Knock, knock," said someone on the back porch.

I spun around and saw Dallas.

Grinning, he said, "Hi. Sounds like a barnyard in there."

My heart fluttered as I grinned back. "Come on in."

"Hi, boy," said Reenie.

Dallas tipped an imaginary hat to her, then opened the screen door and sauntered in. His grin widened as he opened a book and pointed out a paragraph. "Read this."

I read the words quickly to myself: "The Germans began making feather trees in the last half of the nineteenth century. The heavy wire branches were tightly wrapped with goose feathers, which had been boiled to remove the oil, then dyed a dark green. Early trees had round bases painted red or white, often embellished with flecks of gold paint. . . ."

I stopped reading and looked at Dallas. "That sounds like Reenie's tree."

"If it's a genuine antique, the going rate's a hundred dollars a foot."

And we had a two-foot tree in the dining room. Two hundred dollars! "But who—why?"

"Collectors. I told you they don't care about the price. They want what they want, and they have to have it."

My brain started clicking, figuring ways to cash in on the tree. Two hundred smackeroos or two hundred rocks—they were all the same to Reenie. Still, it was her tree.

"Have you read up on the buttons yet?" Dallas asked.

"I've been too busy." Duh. Not very convincing, considering the nail file in my hand. "I—uh—we just caught a humongous blacksnake. It's in a barrel in the barn."

Dallas's eyes widened. "No kidding?"

"No kidding."

"Can I see it?"

"Sure."

Reenie walked outside with us, but she wouldn't go near the barn. She propped her See 'n' Say against the piano tree, climbed onto the swing, and began pumping with her spindly legs and crooning about "my boy" and "my swing."

While Dallas marveled at the size of the snake, I stood at least six feet away and tried to look fearless. He didn't need to know that the very thought of the creature gave me the heebie-jeebies.

When Dallas left, I sat on the porch steps with his book and started reading up on buttons. Right away, I spied two pictures that matched a couple of the buttons on Reenie's tree. That little boy-and-girl button was a Hansel and Gretel, worth twelve-fifty. The man with the funny hat was Teddy Roosevelt in Africa, worth twenty-five.

Quickly, I scanned more pages, but I didn't find another match. However, the values were going up with each succeeding page, and my eyes bugged out when I saw some of the prices.

"Balloon race at the 1904 World's Fair, one hundred fifty . . . Little Red Riding Hood, seven hundred . . . Republic of Texas with Lone Star, one thousand . . ."

Incredible! Who would pay that kind of money for a *button*?

Collectors, that's who.

Collectors like Aunt Ruby?

I squinted across the barn lot at the trash Dad hadn't gotten around to burning yet. Topping the pile was the lumber from the hog shed. We'd misjudged the importance of that hog shed in this snaky place. What if we'd misjudged the buttons, too? Could Aunt Ruby have been a genuine collector and the buttons an investment?

I ran to the trash pile and pawed through junk and boxes, stopping only to sneeze now and then from the cloud of dust I was stirring up. I found six buttons, only one of which I'd seen pictured in the book—a celluloid anchor, worth six dollars. But who knew what I might find in the next box? If I came across that Republic of Texas, we'd be rich. Filthy rich.

I laughed. I was already halfway there—filthy. My jeans and sweatshirt were speckled with dirt and bits of postcards.

High up on the heap, the "Texas Grapefruit" box caught my eye. Texas! Maybe that was an omen. Maybe the button I wanted was in that box.

I climbed up, avoiding the rusty spike nails in the boards, and reached for the grapefruit box.

In the next fraction of a second, I heard the crack of lumber splitting and felt the junk under me give way. Clawing madly at thin air, I plunged down, down into blackness.

TWENTY-THREE
The Second Hero

I OPENED MY EYES. I was in Dallas's parlor. No, this hole was much deeper, much darker, and it smelled stagnant, moldy. Overhead, through a jagged opening, I spied a tattered bit of cloud hanging in the sky.

It was cold down here. Cold as a grave.

I cried out—a weak cry, more like a yelp—but it let me know I was alive. If I wasn't dead, this couldn't be a grave.

But why couldn't I move?

My head and shoulders were jammed against something squishy, like mud. My left arm was resting against something hard and flat. As my eyes adjusted to the darkness, I saw I was buried in boxes and boards from my chest down.

It all came back to me. The fall. The fear. The objects crashing down on top of me.

Looking up, I saw more boards teetering dangerously at the top of the hole. I was surrounded by the slimy walls of a cistern or a well.

I tried to pull my right arm out from under the debris. My sleeve was snagged on something, and when it finally came loose, it was dark and wet.

I could taste blood from a cut on my lip, and I assumed that was blood on my sleeve, but I felt no pain.

Now for my left arm. Oh! A board was stuck to my bicep. I was impaled on a nail, spindled like an invoice at a warehouse. It didn't hurt, but the sight made me nauseous. There was hardly any blood—a trickle.

With my right arm, I pushed away some of the junk, then tried to shift my body to a sitting position. A white-hot pain shot through my left leg. I'd never had a broken bone, but I was pretty sure I had one now.

Gently, I lay back against the mud. Even that little movement brought another stab of pain to my leg.

The horror of my predicament began to sink in. It wasn't even noon yet, and I was helpless in this hole. It would be hours before Mom or Dad and Jim Bob came home.

Reenie was out there somewhere—still singing, unaware of my fall. If I could somehow make her hear me, maybe she could dial "O" and ask for help.

No. Even that was hopeless. Aunt Sage had left her phone off the hook.

What would Reenie do when she realized I was gone? Fear surged through me when I remembered I hadn't removed the burner knob from the stove. Would she discover it and play in the fire? Would she strike out down the road in search of me? Would she wander off to Dallas's?

Dallas's. Reenie could find Dallas's house. Even if she couldn't make him understand that I was in trouble, he'd bring her back to me.

"Reenie!" My voice echoed against the dank walls of my prison. Was it loud enough to be heard from outside? Pushing myself up with my right arm, I tried again. "Reenie!" I croaked, then fell back, exhausted, aching.

She didn't stop singing.

I don't know how long I lay there. It seemed like hours. I became aware of a cold dampness saturating my jeans and jacket, and wondered if I was sinking in the mud.

Suddenly, I heard Reenie's gruff voice calling, "S-sissy?"

She'd missed me. She was looking for me. Ignoring the pain, I forced myself up again. "Reenie!"

"This is a kitten." Pause, grind. "Quack-quack, quack-quack."

"Reenie! Here! Down here!"

"S-sissy?"

I couldn't see her yet, but her voice seemed nearer. "I'm down in the hole! Don't come too close, or you might fall in, too!"

Above me, a piece of trash jiggled, so that dirt sifted into my eyes. I blinked it away, not wanting to tear my gaze from the opening. I heard the string of the See 'n' Say being pulled at the same time Reenie's head appeared above me. Her slanty eyes peered down into the darkness. She must have seen me. She froze.

"Reenie, I need help. I need you to get Dallas."

She didn't respond. Her face was expressionless, except for that red Kool-Aid grin I was seeing upside down.

"Reenie, can you get Dallas?"

The See 'n' Say fell from her hands, and I ducked.

"This is a pig: Oink-oink," it said, then cracked me on the head.

My eyes fluttered open. I touched the place where my head was throbbing. It was swollen and sticky.

My vision was blurred. Where was I? Why was I so cold?

I wanted to huddle up close to a fire in the wood stove. I wanted to feel its heat on my face, then turn around and cook my backside.

But I couldn't turn around. I couldn't move. I couldn't get out of this pit.

Pit. Panic swept through me. Was I in a snake pit?

Before my eyes flashed an image of that snake in the barrel. Mouth opening and closing convulsively. Tail lashing.

I shuddered. Don't think about snakes. Snakes are black, cold-blooded. Think about warmth and light. Think about ham and beans simmering on the wood stove. Think about yellow beams from the windows bathing the sagging front porch. Think about Mom and Dad snuggling on the lumpy old couch.

I was sick of looking at these damp walls. Sick of lying in the mud. My strength was waning. Was I bleeding somewhere? Was this what it felt like to bleed to death?

I closed my eyes. Maybe I fell asleep. Maybe I passed out. I awoke with a start that sent a pain like a thousand stinging bumblebees down my left leg.

Where was Reenie? Where was Dallas? Had she found him yet? Or was she wandering around in the woods, as helpless as I?

No, she had the trail of rags. Jiniwin's trail.

That trail seemed a million miles away, as far away as last Saturday.

Last Saturday, when Reenie had first seen the monster snake.

"Don't think about snakes," I said aloud.

I forced my mind in a different direction. School. Miss Molly. D-Day. The living lab. Never again would I be afraid of a little old baby boa in a cage. But there I was, thinking about snakes again.

Focus on Reenie. Is she all right? What if Dallas isn't home and she tries to light his kerosene lamp? Or what if she hurries too much and her heart acts up? No, no. She's Mom's Humpty Dumpty baby—all put together again. She's survived all the obstacles, just like that tree in the silo. Please, God, don't let Humpty Dumpty break because of me.

Voices? Did I hear voices? I held my breath and

listened. Yes, Dallas was saying, "Careful, Reenie. Stay back."

I saw his head, then Reenie's, upside down. My sister had saved me. I wanted to cry, but I was too weak for tears.

"Buddy, are you hurt?" asked Dallas.

"Yes. I broke my leg, I think."

"I'll call the rescue squad."

"The phone doesn't work."

"Then I'll run to a neighbor's house. Will you be okay here? Boy, that's dumb. You're stuck here."

"I'll be okay. Reenie'll keep me company, won't you, Reenie?"

"Yeah, s-sissy."

"Dallas, call my mom, too. If she's not at the nursing home, try the school."

"Right."

After Dallas disappeared, Reenie lay down on her belly to watch and wait, her eyes locking with mine across the chasm that separated us. Concern was stamped on her face as plain as the Kool-Aid on her mouth. She looked so small, so scared and vulnerable. I wanted to hold her, comfort her, tell her everything would be all right.

"Thanks, Reenie, for getting Dallas. You're a hero. You know that?"

"Yeah, s-sissy."

An eternity passed before Dallas came back and announced, "Help is on the way."

"Thank you," I whispered. I was cold, so cold.

"How'd you happen to end up down there?"

"The grapefruit box. Texas."

"What?"

"I was looking for the Republic of Texas button. The next thing I knew, the earth opened up."

A paint can toppled into the hole and clanked against a board at my feet, and Dallas said, "Man, this junk is hanging by a thread up here. I'm gonna move it, before any more falls on you. Close your eyes. There'll be a lot of dirt."

I did as he asked. I could hear him muttering to himself as he extracted lumber from the heap.

It was crazy, but I felt safer now, and I let my consciousness slip away.

TWENTY-FOUR
The Pumpkin

THAT TATTERED BIT OF CLOUD was spinning and spinning, sucking me so high up into its whirlwind that my eyes hurt from the sun.

"She's coming around."

I peeked through the slits of my eyes. The sun was blinding me, but oh, its warmth was heavenly. How strange. Up close, the sun looked like a giant headlight, and it gave off a scent of cool, minty medicine.

"More glucose. And get her typed immediately, in case she needs blood."

"Yes, Doctor."

I smiled. If I'd died and gone to heaven, I at least had a doctor who wanted to bring me back to life.

I awoke in a criblike bed with metal rails. Nursery rhyme characters smiled down at me from the ceiling.

It seemed as though I'd been lying on my back

forever, and I tried to roll over. I couldn't. I was too weak, too groggy. Both my arms were bandaged, and stuck in my left wrist was a needle hooked up to a plastic tube. The tube was attached to a bag of clear liquid hanging on a rack beside my bed. My left leg was elevated, and I lifted the covers and saw a cast on my leg below the knee.

"She's waking up, Irene."

I turned to see both my parents hustling toward my bed. They looked washed out, older—maybe because my vision was still blurry.

"Oh, Buddy," Mom breathed, her voice cracking. "We were so scared."

Dad smiled and patted my hand. "Not half as scared as you were, though, I'll bet."

"Dad—" I swallowed. My lip was puffy, my throat dry. "Dad, Reenie saved me."

"I know, hon. Our little Reenie's a hero." His smile faded. "I'm so sorry, hon. I had no idea those rotten boards were covering a cistern."

I felt cold again, as if I were still trapped underground. "I kept imagining that hole was a snake pit."

"No wonder," said Mom. "Reenie showed us the monster in the barrel."

"You'll have to tell me how you did that," Dad said.

Mom touched his arm. "Not now, James. The IV is keeping her doped up. That concussion was mild, but still, she needs her rest."

Concussion? My hand went to my head, and I felt

another bandage where the See 'n' Say had landed. "Where's Reenie?"

"Home," Mom said. "Jim Bob and Dallas are staying with her. It'll take both of them to keep track of her."

"Hope they don't blink," I murmured. The talking was wearing me out.

I drifted off again, and when I woke up, Mom and I were alone.

"Where's Dad?"

"He went home for a while. He'll be back later."

I slept off and on until dark. Although a nurse had removed my IV, I was still groggy when Dad walked into the room, all smiles.

"What's got you grinning like the Cheshire Cat?" asked Mom.

"Buttons," he said, bending to kiss my forehead.

Buttons. My search for them seemed so long ago and far away.

"Seems our daughter here was looking for the Republic of Texas before she fell in the cistern."

"James, you're talking in riddles," said Mom.

Dad explained, then turned back to me. "The boys went through the trash with a fine-toothed comb. They didn't find Texas, but they found some other collectibles. In the morning, I'm going to see a button dealer. We've got six one-piece thirties and—"

"What in the world are one-piece thirties?" interrupted Mom.

"Celluloid buttons made in the nineteen-thirties.

Worth about eight dollars apiece. We've also got some Japanese porcelains and—"

"Fine," Mom said, "but let's not talk about this right now. I don't want Buddy getting all worked up."

She needn't have worried. All I wanted to do was sleep.

Dad stayed for a half hour or so, holding my hand in his big palm, which felt pleasantly rough from the calluses coming back. I drifted off again.

When I woke up, Dad was gone and the room was dark, except for a Mickey Mouse night-light plugged into the wall. Mom, twisted like a pretzel, was snoozing in a chair.

Sometime in the night, a nurse came in and checked my temperature and blood pressure. After she left, I studied Mom, whose soft snores reminded me of Tripod purring. It was obvious she'd dressed in a hurry. She was wearing navy slacks, a green-and-yellow sweater, and her white hose and nurse's shoes.

She should be home in bed, I thought.

Home. That was the first time I'd used the word to describe Aunt Ruby's house.

I tried to picture the witch's head, but I saw only smoke curling along the roof line. I tried to picture the burning eye, but I saw only an oval window bathing the front porch in yellow.

Warmth and light.

I imagined Reenie's face peering down at me, full of warmth and light and hope and love.

Then I saw Jiniwin, standing alone in her doorway, framed by the stained-glass jewels. The picture faded, and I saw Dallas, content in his storm cellar with little more than his independence and self-esteem.

All at once, I was grateful to have parents who cared and a roof over my head—even if it was just an old farmhouse with mice in the window seat and snakes in the oven.

I felt suspended in time, in limbo between the person I was a week ago and the person I was at this moment. Turning my face to the wall, I pretended to sleep, so if Mom woke up, she wouldn't know I was crying.

The doctor came in at sunup. He checked me over and said I could go home after breakfast, if I would take it easy for a few days.

"No problem," I said. "Every muscle in my body is stiff and sore."

"You'll loosen up when you get to moving around. I molded a knob at the bottom of your cast for walking, but I don't want you square dancing for a while."

He helped me out of bed, so I could try out my cast. My trip to the door and back felt like a mile, and when the doctor left, I crawled gratefully back under the covers.

As Mom pushed the button to crank up the bed, she said, "It's a good thing you had an accident, instead of appendicitis."

"What?"

She grinned. "With that school policy, accidents are covered. Illnesses aren't."

The worry lines showed in her forehead, and she'd tried to tame her wiry red hair by dampening it. I thought of myself, lying in the mud, and said, "I bet I'm a scary sight."

"You look beautiful to me. Yesterday, when you were in that hole . . ." Mom shivered, then hugged me, awkwardly, because of my injured arms. "That's a sight a mother can never forget. It's too much like seeing your daughter in a grave."

"Mom, I—I'm really sorry I was so hardheaded about moving. Until I was trapped in that cistern, I didn't see just how good I've got it on the outside."

"I think that's human nature—to not truly appreciate what you have until it's jeopardized. Believe me, it was going through my mind yesterday that maybe I've shortchanged you. Maybe I've given Reenie too much attention and not enough to you."

"It's all right, Mom. It had to be that way. I've been watching over Reenie, too, her whole life. It seems strange that yesterday she was watching over me."

"We've all underestimated Reenie. She's growing up, becoming her own person. She's not my Humpty Dumpty baby anymore. She proved it yesterday by fetching Dallas."

"She proved it twice. She came right out into the yard and helped with the monster."

"You're her idol. She'd do anything for you."

"Except stop playing with fire and running off."

We laughed, and Mom held me tighter. I felt warm, protected, closer to her than I ever had. "Mom, can I tell you something?"

"Sure, hon. Anything."

"It's about Jiniwin. She's been drinking."

"Drinking?" Mom let go of me and looked into my eyes. "Are you sure?"

"I'm sure."

Mom shook her head sadly and sighed. "Paulette's been asking for trouble with Jiniwin for a long time. She's always been wrapped up in herself, but now it's getting worse, and Jiniwin's the one who has to suffer."

"What can we do?"

"I'll talk to her. She needs to get herself and Jiniwin into counseling."

"What if she won't listen?"

"She'll listen, or I'll report her to the authorities for child neglect. Being a court reporter, she knows the legal ramifications, and she'd hate to have to answer to a judge."

Dad came to take us home about ten o'clock. He whispered something to Mom, and they both laughed and looked smug, but they wouldn't let me in on the mystery.

A nurse took me downstairs in a wheelchair. Dad lifted me into the car and got me situated with my left leg stretched out on the backseat.

We drove through Turnback and passed the flea

market at the fairgrounds. The day was cloudy, the wind icy, but that hadn't discouraged the bargain hunters. They were out in full force, and I wasn't able to spot Dallas in the crowd.

A mile farther on, I saw the silo with the tree sticking out. The leaves, leaning in the wind, seemed to be directing us to the farm.

As Dad turned west onto the gravel road, I looked back at the blacktop going north. This evening, especially for Reenie, I'd ask Dad to take us on the countrified version of a trip around the horn.

I found myself watching for landmarks. Three farmhouses, two barns, then the turn onto the gravel road leading *home*. I smiled. It wasn't just Aunt Ruby's house any longer. It was my home, my pumpkin, and I couldn't wait to see it.

There was Dallas's mailbox. I wondered just how long he could keep his secret. Sooner or later, someone in my family was bound to drop in on him. If not Mom with a cake or a casserole, then Jim Bob offering a ride in the pickup.

What would happen then? I didn't know, but I had a feeling my parents would do everything they could to see that Dallas had a proper place to live. It even crossed my mind that Aunt Sage might take him in. Probably neither she nor Dallas would admit it, but they both needed someone to look after them. They could look after each other.

Dad was slowing down for the cattle guard. Ahead,

I saw smoke curling from the chimney, along the roof, down the porch pole to the ground.

"When the smoke drifts low, the weather's changing," said Dad.

I barely heard him. I was zeroed in on Jim Bob, Reenie, and Dallas, who had just come bursting out the front door. "Why isn't Dallas at the flea market?"

"He wanted to be here when you came home," Dad replied.

I was surprised and touched, because I knew how much Dallas needed money, and in only a couple of weeks the flea market would be closing for the season.

Dallas's bike, minus the cart, was standing in the yard. Tied to the handlebars was a red-and-white-striped bakery bag, the kind they used at the Soda Jerk.

When the car stopped, my welcoming committee yanked open the doors. Jim Bob and Dallas said "Hi," and helped me get out. Reenie planted a kiss on my cheek, and said, "My s-sissy. My girl."

The boys made a chair with their arms and carried me into the house. I breathed deeply, savoring the smell of wood heat and the lingering scent of breakfast bacon.

In the kitchen, Tripod was grooming himself on an overstuffed chair that had been moved in close to the wood stove. Reenie's red and yellow and blue flags looped out and up from the ceiling light to all four corners of the room. On the table sat a vase of goldenrod and a plate of doughnuts. Recalling the bakery bag on Dallas's bike, I knew he'd ridden to town to buy them.

"My flags," said Reenie proudly.

I glanced from her to Dallas to Jim Bob. It was hard to talk past the knot in my throat. "You did all this for me?"

"My s-sissy," said Reenie. The guys grinned sheepishly.

With a gentle nudge of his tennis shoe, Jim Bob shooed Tripod out of the chair, and he and Dallas eased me into it. I squeezed my brother's shoulder gratefully, and he grinned at me and winked. He'd never had a better reason for calling me Ella-Short-for-Elephant, but he'd let the opportunity pass.

"Thought you'd want to be where the action is," he said as Tripod jumped into my lap. "We moved your bed into the dining room."

I glanced in at my bed and nightstand, at a neat row of rocks on the windowsill, at the feather tree on the chair. That tree belonged there, and I was certain I'd never want to sell it. Ducking my head, I petted the purring Tripod. His brain-colored fur was a blob before my watery eyes, and I blinked rapidly to clear them.

"Have you told her yet?" asked Dallas.

"No," said Dad. "I wanted everybody together when I broke the news."

"What news?" I asked.

"About my visit with the dealer." A smile lit up

Dad's face as he fiddled with the flap on his pocket. This time, the pocket wasn't empty, and he pulled out a folded blue paper.

It was a check, and I could tell by the excited faces around me that it must be a sizable one. But it didn't matter now whether we had money or not. The important thing was having my family around me, having their love. I felt my face flush. How many times had I grouched about moving to the farm? How many times had I muttered the hateful phrase, "When pigs fly"?

"Besides the one-piece thirties and the Japanese porcelains," Dad said, "we found some Silver Millers."

"Studio buttons," explained Dallas. "Made by a fellow named Miller early in the century."

"Couldn't prove it by me," Dad chuckled. "All I know is those beauties were worth a hundred fifty dollars apiece. But the real prize was that George Washington inaugural button worth nine hundred bucks." His eyes flashing with merriment, he held up the check so I could read it. One thousand, eight hundred fourteen dollars.

My heart skipped a beat. "That's enough, isn't it, Dad? Enough to keep you from welding on those tanks?"

"This definitely takes the pressure off, but with you getting hurt, I'd already decided that being on the road's not for me. There are things in life lots more important than a big paycheck. I'll keep doing odd jobs, and we'll use this windfall to pay off a few bills."

"Tell her about the barbed wire," said Dallas.

Dad seized him playfully at the back of the neck. "This young fellow knows his wire. We found some really old pieces in the barn. Valuable, if we find the right collector. In the spring, we'll buy some hogs and raise a litter or two of pigs. Money in the bank, if the market stays up."

"Not to mention that they'll kill snakes," said Mom, and we all laughed.

Reenie, eager for my attention, stuck the See 'n' Say in my face and pulled the string.

Tripod yowled and sailed off my lap as the mechanical voice said, "This is a turkey. . . ."

Suddenly, I remembered the See 'n' Say plummeting down into the hole and conking me on the head. The pig had *oinked,* for once. I laughed out loud. The pig had flown! That was one for the history books—or at least for the writing wall.

"Where you going?" asked Mom, because I'd heaved myself out of the chair and was clumping across the kitchen.

"Have to record a moment in history," I said as I grabbed for the pen by the telephone. I'd moved too fast, and I was woozy. When I stumbled against the cabinet, Dallas caught my elbow to steady me.

He helped me along as I hobbled to the dining room and stopped in front of the writing wall. High up, as far as I could reach, I drew a huge pumpkin and scribbled inside it, "THE PIG FLIES! October 14."

"What's that supposed to mean?" Dallas asked.

I leaned heavily against him, exhausted again. "It's a secret," I whispered. "Tell you later."

"I'm the world's best at keeping secrets," he said. Then he grinned and zipped his lip.